Praise for the 13 Reasons for Murder Series

"…hard to put down and am keen to read the next in the series."—Reader's Favorite 5-Star

"Full of sass, good friends, and a bit of blood, this novel was a joy to read."—Julie E.

"…suspenseful, addictive…hope there are more books with this character."—BookBub Review

"I look forward to…learning more about Britney."—Studiohnh.com Review

"…oddly addictive…cannot wait for the next book…"—Amazon.ca Review

"…flows at a quick pace and leaves you wanting more…"—Goodreads Review

"The plot is fresh and unique, a nice change to read something a little different…"—Reader's Favorite 4-Star

"…well written and kept me on the edge of my seat…"—Heather W.

13 Reasons for Murder: Hungry

13 Reasons for Murder #4

Amanda Byrd

Blacksheep Press

About the
Author

Amanda has a love of horror and borderline obsession with fictional serial killers. She frequently makes *Hannibal*, *Harry Potter*, and *Dexter* references in "normal" conversation. She is also a full-time psychology major. When not writing, Amanda can be found reading, playing video games, or watching shows and movies like *Mindhunter*, *Hannibal*, *Harry Potter,* or *Dexter*. Amanda currently resides in Tampa, Florida with her husband and two cats.

Follow Amanda online: www.amandabyrd.net
Sign up for the monthly email list and get a free story

Contents

For you on the frontlines of everyday life.
Thank you for doing what the rest of us cannot.

One

SHAE AND I TALKED a lot after our last lunch. Well, sort of. Most of it was day-to-day nonsense, not the kind of talking we started at lunch. Was she embarrassed? Or hiding something? It was probably a combination of both. I know I didn't enjoy opening up about the stalker thing to those who didn't already know. "The Crazy Flame" was decidedly the worst nickname ever, and it hadn't worn off yet. Fuck the media. Assholes.

Danielle called one day to ask about Shae and how the two of us were getting along.

"Fine," I said. "Shae's pretty much on this planet and decent. But I don't know her all that well either. Is everything okay?"

"Yeah. I was just wondering is all." Danielle sighed. "She finally took over all the way. The bosses aren't her biggest fans, but she does such a great job. I guess it's her personality they don't like so much."

"What about her personality? I don't see anything wrong."

"Well, she's pretty blunt, like you. That may be why you see nothing wrong."

I thought about that for a minute, not saying anything. Danielle sucked her breath in. I guess she was afraid she insulted or offended me. Fat chance. The media offended me, my friends did not. They should know they could be honest with me. Danielle is the one friend who sometimes gets weird about full honesty, which is understandable. None of us wants to upset anyone without cause.

"Fair point," I responded, "I am pretty brutal sometimes, especially around friends. Want me to talk to her?"

I heard an excited gasp on the other end of the line.

"Could you please? I mean, if it's not too much trouble."

"Of course I can, Danielle. We've been friends how long? You know you can ask me anything." I smiled as I spoke, hoping she'd hear it in my tone.

"I do. I just get so, I don't know, weird, sometimes."

"We all do," I quipped. We both laughed.

"I'm supposed to see her for lunch again next week. I can talk to her then. Or is that too late?"

"No, that's great. They're not ready to fire her or anything. They're just concerned. Thanks, Brit. This means a lot."

"No thanks needed, girl. Please know you can come to me about anything."

"I know. I still get weird asking others, too, so it's not just you. I'm getting better, though."

"You are and I'm proud to call you my friend. So, when are me and you gonna have lunch?"

"Hmm, let me check my schedule…" Her voice drifted away and came back. "How does Wednesday sound?"

I looked at my planner. "Wednesday sounds perfect! You choose time and place."

"Cool. I'll let you know tomorrow."

"Great. Chat soon!"

I pressed the "end" button on my phone and smiled. We'd been friends for over twenty years, and I didn't change much during that time. Danielle, though, had grown considerably.

She used to be so timid, and now she puts her foot down. She can even be mean when she has to be. I adore her.

As for my friendship with the others, Sarah had been the longest. We've known each other twenty-five or so years. It felt like so much less time had gone by, but we knew how old we really were and when we'd met. Yes, we were toddlers. Life is crazy sometimes, and having excellent friends makes it more tolerable.

The girls still asked how I was doing after the stalker incidents. They didn't mean anything other than who they knew me to be—a 27-, almost 28-year-old woman, living alone with a cat who only knew how to defend herself in close quarters or by brains. It had to stay that way, no matter how much more difficult it got.

Keeping my secret sometimes felt like a chore; sometimes I wanted to share my kills with someone. I couldn't. Ever. This is my life, not some TV show that was based on a book series and chose to wildly diverge from the precise path of the books to become its own thing. I also sometimes think the author of those books followed me and based his killer on me, but that would be absurd. Right?

I finished entering a new hire into the system and shut down for the day. Barb had already been taking messages for me, telling clients I was in a meeting. Of course I wasn't, but I also wasn't in a mood to be talking to them. I was irrational and easy to irritate. No, it's not PMS. It's just today's mood.

I knew I had to call my therapist, Ben, and talk to him about it. He'd probably refer me to a shrink, and that thought didn't sit well. What else was I supposed to do? I didn't want meds, but I was starting to unhinge, and I'd get caught if I got any worse. Doctor-patient privilege doesn't cover this, so I have to be sly talking about it.

After shutting my computer down, I gathered my things and walked out of my office, closing the door behind me. Barb looked up from her screen and smiled at me. I smiled back and waved "bye." She returned the wave as I walked out the front door.

After I climbed into the driver's seat, I took my jacket off and shifted into drive. Then pulled out of my parking space and up to the light that granted my exit onto Waters Avenue. The drive home wasn't as crowded as usual—it was only 2 p.m.

I said I wasn't in any kind of mood to be working today and I meant it. Every minor thing got on my nerves, and I suspected that my anxiety was starting to rear its ugly head. It hadn't been a problem since high school; I'd learned how to manage my control issues then. My inability to control other people—and the cops—must be what caused the anxiety to start coming back.

The thought that it crept back into my life annoyed me to no end. I hated it. Alternative coping methods were acceptable and welcome. Anything more than that is not. I've heard horror stories about anxiety, and I've experienced my own. Once, I even had a blackout from stress and anxiety. I'm still only remembering bits and pieces of those six months.

I kept driving south, past the roads I usually take to get home—past my house. I drove to the parking lot for the beach and parked. I took my shoes off and got out of my Jeep. I stood there for a minute, soaking in the sights and smells and heat. My feet were cooler here on the asphalt than they'd be on the sand, but I walked out onto it anyway. I stopped at the shoreline, letting the water lap up over the tops of my feet. I hate sand so much; it gets in places it should never be. But I allowed myself to feel the squish between my toes until I couldn't handle it anymore.

Back at my Jeep, I pulled a bottle of water out and rinsed the sand from my feet before climbing back in. The sounds of the beach were many—from kids playing to the crash of the waves further out. The bay churned like my mind, yet it was somehow comforting. I backed out of the parking spot and drove home.

Minion greeted me in the kitchen when I came in. Her usual look of judgment and a scream were all it took for me to cave and give her a small bit of food before her regular feeding time. She's so spoiled.

I carried my shoes in my hand up to my bedroom where I changed into pajamas and went back downstairs to just lounge and read or watch TV. Then my phone rang. The caller ID displayed Shae's name and number.

"Hey girl!"

"Brit, I need your help."

Two

SHAE HAD BEEN RAMBLING for close to twenty minutes about work and how one of her bosses made a comment about tact. I guessed that Danielle may have been wrong about the time frame. Shit.

"Shae, breathe. I kind of already knew this was a thing. Danielle called me and asked if I could talk to you about it because I'm the most…qualified, if you will. You already know how blunt I am, and I'm like that mainly with friends. It took a lot of work for me to not come off so rude to clients and employees. Hell, Barb still has an issue getting used to it, and she's been with me how long now? So yeah, I get it."

"But how do I control this? And how do people know I'm not faking nice? Does it even matter? And—"

"Breathe," I interrupted. Shae did.

"But…Britney, you'll really help me? I like my job and don't want to be fired."

"Yes, I'll help you. It's not easy though. Are you ready for the hard work?"

"Damn straight."

"Cool."

For the next thirty minutes, I gave Shae the basics of what she needed to do to address the problem. We talked about how I handle speaking to others. I told her how exhausting it is but also that it needs to be done. Hell, I'd have no clients and no company and no employees if I couldn't manage my seemingly insensitive tone. So, I gave her tips and promised we could role play for her to work on it. I was lucky when I first started working on my manners. I had Joe Osten to guide me, and I knew I should ask for him to help Shae. But I needed to learn more about her and who she was, so I waited.

It was around four when we hung up. I went back to playing with the remote, flipping through shows and movies. Reading wasn't going to happen, and I was okay with that; shows that didn't require my full attention would be perfect right now anyway. I was still feeling weird but there wasn't much I could do about it, other than let it run its course. I'd be back to myself tomorrow.

I clicked to some mini-series documentary about someone hoarding cats and pressed play. The next three hours were like watching a dumpster fire roll right onto train tracks and get smashed by the locomotive. That was all I could handle before I started to get hungry. I ordered delivery from a local bar with amazing Cuban sandwiches and got back to the mind-numbingly batshit story. These people were all insane, to varying degrees. It made me feel so much better about my current state of mental unravel.

The doorbell rang, telling me my dinner had arrived. I answered the door, tipped the driver, and took my food back to the couch to continue this insanity. I didn't know how I was able to watch so much of it, but I was grateful for the escape. Tomorrow would bring me back to reality. Tonight, I enjoyed my food and relaxed. Minion tried to steal some of my sandwich but was unsuccessful and decided to beg for scraps instead. I laughed and gave her a small piece of the bread. She barely chewed and started begging again, but I wasn't having it. She's spoiled enough.

Out of the seven total episodes of the show, I finished four before going to bed. On my way upstairs, I texted Julie, asking if she'd seen it yet. By the time I climbed into bed, Julie hadn't responded, which I expected. She was likely asleep. Though I suspected Brain, her son, was awake reading. We shared the same interest in books, and when one of us found a new favorite author or series, we would tell the other one about it. It was kind of like a secret book club, and me and Brian were the only members. As I laid my head on my pillow and started to drift off, Minion landed inches from my face and dug her way under the blanket to her cuddle spot.

• • • ● • ● ● • • •

I woke to a message from Julie.

Hahaha! I've seen it. AWFUL!

I laughed and replied.

Lunch today to discuss?

After I hit send, I tossed the blanket off me and got ready for my day. It would be a long one, full of returning emails and calls and doing everything I didn't want to do yesterday.

Barb was already at her desk working when I walked in around 8:30.

"Wow, you're early today," I commented.

"I was hoping to fill you in on yesterday before you got started."

"Oh? Is everything okay?"

Barb blushed. "Yes. Nothing to worry about. But I think that accounting guy—the one you placed while you were looking for a new assistant?—was flirting with me. I mean, I think he thought I was Julie."

"Oh wow! Barb, I'm so sorry! I'll call him and fix this. Would you be opposed to him calling to apologize?"

"Not at all. But, between you and me, I kind of hope he knew it was me and meant it. He's a decent guy and I *am* single." She blushed again. I giggled.

"So you don't want me to call him?"

"No, let's see what happens."

"Okay, Barb. I won't call him." I winked and walked away.

I set my things down in their usual places and booted up my computer. I'm a creature of habit when it comes to work. And I'm well organized—everything has an exact place. I mean, yeah, I'm organized at home too, but more so at the office. One of my many quirks.

Time flew by, with me on the phone more than I ever imagined I could be in such a short period. I felt my right ear growing warmer as I put the receiver down in its cradle. Then the pain started. I checked off half a dozen names on the list I'd written for myself. I sighed and opened my email application and started replying to some outstanding emails, giving my ear a break.

The next thing I knew, Barb was standing in the doorway saying something about what time it was. I shook my head as I pulled away from the screen.

"I'm sorry, I didn't hear you. Can you repeat that?"

Barb laughed. "I said it's lunch time."

"Oh wow. Okay then. Thanks. I take it—"

"—Yes, I've learned how you are when you're focused," she finished for me.

I laughed. "At least I wasn't drooling." Barb laughed with me.

I stood and grabbed my purse, checking my phone on the way out. Barb waved as I left. I checked my phone on the short walk to my Jeep, seeing that Julie responded with a place.

I turned onto N. Dale Mabry and parked at the restaurant inside of ten minutes. That must have been a record. I hopped out and hugged Julie at the door. We walked into The Broken Yolk Cafe and were seated by the friendly brunette at the door.

The door dinged a few times and we thought nothing of it. Then I heard his voice.

Three

"IT'S SO GOOD TO see you, Britney!"

I jumped from my seat, spinning in the air, attack-hugging Cody.

"Oh my God! Where have you been? It feels like forever! How are you? Jesus." I paused for a breath. "Sit. Then tell me everything I've missed."

Cody walked to the other side of the table, sitting next to Julie. He kissed her cheek and started talking. They completed each other's sentences and talked excitedly about Brian and wedding planning and Cody's job.

"I got an internship at one of the top firms in Tampa," Cody excitedly said.

"Celebratory dinner, got it," I replied, raising my glass of iced tea in toast.

Julie and Cody raised their glasses and we clinked.

Cody thanked me. "Brit, you don't need to do that."

"I want to. This is a big deal. You've worked so hard for this."

"I know, but…can we make it just us, please? Maybe at home?"

I smiled wide. "Of course! I'll bring the food and we can eat with our hands for all I care."

We haven't had a dinner comprised of just us in a few weeks. Basically since Julie opened the office. I thought I might bring it up at Cody's celebration dinner. Timing for that sort of thing wasn't an issue—they knew me well enough to know I pointed out observations as I could.

We ordered, ate, and caught up on all the important things we'd missed in the time since we last enjoyed a meal together. We laughed until it hurt and had a great time.

Then the lunch hour was over, Julie and I needing to get back to our respective offices. We all hugged and set a day and time for dinner before getting into our vehicles and parting ways. It felt so good to see Julie and Cody that I teared up a little as I pulled out of the lot. I missed them and Brian so much. Sure, I texted with them, but it wasn't the same.

Back at the office, Barb was back at her desk before I walked in. I felt that something was off, so I asked her.

"Barb, is everything okay? This is twice today that you've been at your desk before I even get here."

"Oh yes, I'm great." She smiled. With my being used to lies and the telltale signs of such things, I looked for hers. There wasn't one. She was being truthful.

"Okay," I said, cocking my head a little, "if you need to talk, I'm not just your boss, you know."

"I do. Thanks, Britney."

I smiled. "No need for thanks."

Barb blushed as I walked back to my desk.

The day dragged on, with moments of me losing focus just enough to feel the pangs of misery caused by missing my favorite people. Who am I becoming? Or what? I'm not supposed to have feelings like this. I'm a killer, for shit's sake.

I pounded the keyboard, finishing the email I was replying to, and clicked send with such ferocity, I thought I may have broken the mouse. Then I picked up my cell phone and typed in a name.

"Dr. Ben Peterson."

"Ben, it's Britney." I fought hard to not let the anxiety be heard.

"Hey, Brit! What's up?"

"When do you have time for me? I could use a session."

"Are you okay?"

"Maybe? More frustrated than anything."

"Wanna tell me what's going on? Maybe I can help now instead of later."

This is why he's my therapist. He'll still charge me, but no trip to his office.

I huffed, then spoke. "Well, it seems I have feelings."

Ben burst into laughter for a good minute before he calmed down enough to talk. "You think having feelings is…a problem?"

"When have you known me to be upset about not seeing friends and family? Better yet, when have you known me to care about someone enough to consider having a romantic relationship with them?"

I thought I heard him spit out a drink.

"I'm sorry, say that again."

"You heard me. Now just isn't the time for me to be dating anyone, and he respects that. But seriously, Ben. Feelings. What is wrong with me?"

"I think your anxieties are helping to push your feelings toward the surface."

"That's it?"

"You ask as though it's a simple fix. Brit, there's no switch to turn it off. It's not a light."

"Fuck," I spat. "There has to be a way to silence them."

"You could try mindfulness."

"Details please?"

For the next twenty minutes, Ben told me the basics of mindfulness and suggested different resources to help me out. I thanked him and we hung up. My email dinged two minutes later—Ben's bill. I opened it and shook my head. He didn't charge me. As in zero.

Then I went online and searched bookstores for the workbooks he recommended and bought all of them. I need this problem squashed. Fast.

I finished placing the order and got back to work. I only had a few calls and emails left. I was surprised that it took me all day to get through them. After clicking the send button on the last email, I went back over my list to make sure I didn't miss anything. That's when I realized how much I got done. Sometimes, I even impress myself.

Today was a good day. I needed it. Then again, I could use a few more, especially to work on shutting my feelings off. Or maybe I could calm them down to a more acceptable volume. I kind of like knowing I'm not the heartless bitch I see in the mirror.

I gathered my things and turned my computer off. Barb was packing her things to head home.

"Barb, how was your day? I feel like shit for not being available."

"You're fine." She waved me off. "Jim called again."

"Jim." I tried to recall who she meant. "Jim who?"

"The accountant-slash-CFO guy you placed at one of the law offices."

"Oh! And?"

"He flirted again. I'm too nervous to ask if he realizes it's me he's talking to."

"Barbara," —I walked to her desk, set my things down, and placed my hands on her shoulders— "You're beautiful.

You're shy too, and I understand that. It's part of why I hired you. I know you can be a lion when you need to, or even when you just want to. I was like you once." I wasn't, but it made her smile.

"Brit…I-I don't know…"

"Yes you do. Think about what you want and go from there. If you want to try dating him, do it. If not, don't. I know I make it sound easy. I believe in you and you do too." I winked. "You've got more courage inside of you than you realize." I hugged her, said goodnight, and left.

Traffic on the way home was almost as light as it was at lunch. I didn't hear about anything happening that would have shut roads down, though it was a really great day for the beach. And the people of the Tampa Bay Area lived their lives around beach days.

When I got home, I was greeted at the door by Minion and her pitiful meows. It wasn't quite her feeding time, so I scooped her up in my arms. She screamed a bit more, then settled onto my shoulder, and purred. She's such a needy little girl and it's probably my fault. Whatever.

I'd made it up the stairs to my bedroom to change, where Minion leaped off my shoulder and onto the bed; carrying her like a child only lasted so long. I was happy because it meant I could change and not have my back torn to shreds. Which also meant no blood on my clothes. I really didn't need to be taking things to the dry cleaner asking them to get the blood out. I've been lucky and careful so far. Maybe I'd look into one of those plastic suits Hannibal had in the TV show. Or a rubber apron. Those were fairly easy to get and inconspicuous.

As I was pulling on pajama pants, the doorbell rang. I growled and yelled down.

"One minute!"

I can only imagine the look on my face when I opened the door in an irritated shock.

Four

MY FACE DIDN'T HAVE an "inside voice." And I was fairly sure the person it was screaming at was either amused or confused. His face wore an expression of pure aloofness until he couldn't hold it anymore and burst into a fit of laughter.

"You should see your face right now," he said between breaths.

"Well, I can't, and now it's too late for you to take a picture," I grumbled, stepping back, and inviting Stu in. "Why are you here?"

He eyed me from my feet up. "I was going to take you to dinner, but you look like you're ready for bed."

"I'm comfortable. And tired. I'll have dinner with you"—I raised an eyebrow and smirked—"if we can order in. Thai."

Stu laughed. "Nothing but your favorite."

I jumped like a child and hugged him. "What did I do to deserve a man like you in my life?"

You lied, you shot a cop and sent him to prison, you continue to lie…and you fell in love with this poor man you'll always lie to. I shook the thoughts away as best as I could before I started to tear up. I fought the rising anger. Stu saw my face twist.

"You okay?"

"Yeah, I'm good," I lied. Damn near everything out of my mouth to this man was a fucking lie. I hated it. And there I go feeling things again. I wanted to scream, to break things, to stab someone.

"One of the delivery apps?" Stu was looking at his phone, opening them to find which one delivered from Northdale to South Tampa.

"No, I'll go get it." I needed to get out so I could scream in the confines of my Jeep.

"Brit, you're in pajamas. I'll go," he offered.

"It's okay. They've totally seen me like this before." We laughed. I felt like I might be starting to relax, but my brain was screeching, on the verge of causing a migraine. Those mindfulness books couldn't get here fast enough.

Stu sat on the couch, looking at the menu to decide what he wanted. Then he looked at me wearing a weird expression.

"What?"

"I wanted to buy dinner." His voice carried a tone of dejection.

"Well, then, you call to place the order, and tell them I'm the one picking it up. They should be okay with that," I said as I sat next to him, pen in hand.

I leaned over to the notepad on the coffee table and started writing.

"Whoa! You don't need the menu?"

I laughed again. "When you order from them as much as I do…"

Stu laughed and shook his head.

We both wrote our orders on the page, and then Stu called.

He hit the end button, looked at me, and said, "Forty-five minutes."

"Sweet!" I grabbed the remote and started flipping through the streaming apps to find something we'd be okay starting and holding off on finishing or something we've already seen and could watch again. A comic book TV show won out. We both enjoyed it, and it was also mindless entertainment…sort of. Like most humans, I yelled at certain characters and cheered when they were killed off. Then again, I cheered when anyone was killed off in any show or movie. The weapons in this show intrigued me, and I wanted to learn the basics of using them, maybe to someone's ultimate end.

I checked my watch to see that twenty-three minutes had passed. I stood and started walking to the door.

"Okay, I'll be back in a bit," I told Stu as I put my shoes on and grabbed my purse.

"I'll keep Minion safe," he joked.

I opened the door and Stu remembered something. "Brit, what about drinks?"

"There's beer and wine in the fridge. And some unsweet tea. And I think that's it."

He fished in his pocket and handed me forty dollars. "Here, maybe grab some beer and soda?"

"Anything specific, Mr. Bud Light?" I smirked.

"Nah. Your choice."

I shrugged, bent down, kissed his cheek, and almost fell into his lap. I'd lost my footing trying to break into a run back to the door. We both blushed and I left.

I was on N. Dale Mabry before I let the scream out. It was so loud, the windows vibrated, and the guy driving the pick-up next to me looked at me, terrified. Then I burst into tears. I wanted to *be* with Stu. I wanted him to be my happy ending; the kind I saw in movies. I knew it wasn't possible—with anyone, ever. I couldn't remember ever wanting something that I couldn't have, let alone how bad I wanted Stu.

"Get it together, Brit. Settling down isn't for you unless it's in prison."

I parked outside the Thai place and went in, eyes misty. I faked a smile when greeted by the hostess who gave me our food. Then I went to the convenience store next door for beer and soda. Two 6-packs of Bud Light, one of Blue Moon, and a few 2 liters of Coke Zero later, I left. Don't judge me. It tastes better than the full sugar version.

I guess Stu heard me backing into the driveway because he was at the driver's side door faster than I could see. He took the beer and soda while I carried the food. Inside, we set everything on the kitchen table so we could put it on plates and get to it easier. I grabbed plates and the necessary silverware and set those on the table, making it look like a buffet. That is, after all, what it was. Stu motioned for me to go first, and, for once, I didn't argue. I filled my plate and grabbed a Blue Moon before heading to the living room.

While Stu plated his food, I cleaned the coffee table off so we had a little more room. I'd even gotten new handmade coasters with really cool and trippy versions of the Cheshire Cat, Maleficent, Ursula, and Cruella de Vil. There was another set with more cartoon villains I had on my list to order next.

Stu came in carrying a plate and a Bud Light, and I laughed.

"What?" he asked with a laugh that was laced with defen-siveness.

I just shook my head.

He sat and handed me a napkin. I took his beer and placed it on the Cruella coaster.

"Hey! Why her?"

"Because Cheshire Cat is mine tonight." I grinned at him and pressed play on a show we'd both wanted to start watching. It was about a man who laundered money for a Mexican cartel.

After we'd finished dinner, Stu took our plates into the kitchen and started washing them. I paused the show and skipped back a few frames so we didn't miss anything. Then I followed Stu, grabbing a towel to dry the dishes with.

Stu looked over at me and smiled. I smiled back, my brain again screaming at me and arguing with my heart. Is this how normal people live? It's fucking bullshit. Now I think I get why people snap. Between my brain yelling and my heart punching my brain, I sure felt like I was about to. I stifled a scream, my face reddening. Stu saw itas he was drying his hands.

He put his hands on my shoulders and looked me in the eyes.

"Brit, are you okay?"

I hung my head, wanting to lie. "No."

I took a few more minutes, a lame attempt to gather my thoughts. "I want to be with you so bad, but I can't."

"It's okay, Brit." Stu's tone was soft and comforting and he wrapped me in a hug.

"I want to be with you, too, but only if you feel it's right."

I buried my face in his shoulder and cried. Stu hugged tighter, kissing the top of my head. He let me cry until I stopped myself a few minutes later. Wiping the tears from my eyes, I pulled back, looked at him, and painted on a smirk.

"More alcohol or will we do something we shouldn't?"

He scratched the back of his head. "Brit…I don't think it's something we shouldn't do. Then again, I don't know why you keep saying you can't be with me."

"I've told you. It's selfish, but my career comes first. Even Julie has taken a bit of a backseat since the new office opened. I just can't manage a relationship right now. I adore you and want to be able to give you more attention than I can now." I hung my head, letting another tear fall.

"I get that, I really do, but"—Stu sighed heavily—"I don't know. I'm trying to stay just friends, but it's so hard."

"I agree. What do we do?" I looked into his eyes and saw the same pain I felt.

"I honestly don't know. Maybe not see each other so often, I guess."

"That would mean you have to stop randomly showing up for dinner." I smiled at him.

"Nah, that just means I can't do it as often." He grinned back.

We sat back on the couch, his arm around me and my head on his shoulder until I fell asleep.

I woke up about an hour later. Stu hadn't moved and was still watching TV. He felt me shift and looked over, smiling.

"Girl, you snore enough to wake the dead!" He pulled his arm away and rubbed it to get rid of the pins and needles.

"I do not!" I responded, wiping drool from my face. "Oh my God, I drooled!"

Stu burst into laughter, tears flowing from his eyes. I joined in. I couldn't remember the last time I drooled, and as embarrassing as it is, it's also pretty funny. I'm just that comfortable around him.

I stood up, shaking my legs out to get the feeling back, and went to grab some wine. I needed to get drunk right about now. Consequences be damned. I came back with a bottle of Jacob's Creek Shiraz and two glasses. Stu shook his head.

"So much for not doing things we shouldn't," he joked.

I poured us each a glass and raised mine in toast.

"To our friendship and whatever else may come. I love you, Stu Jones."

"I love you too, Britney Cage."

We clinked and I chugged. Stu almost spat his out watching me. We finished the first bottle before we even unpaused the show. I grabbed another, and Stu finally took his shoes off and got comfortable. He knew I wasn't about to let him leave drunk. A cop with a DUI is never a good thing. Then again, neither is a serial killer with a cop boyfriend.

I came back, poured us another glass, and sat back. We watched the show and drank another bottle. As I tried to stand to go get yet another bottle, Stu kissed me. Was this what I really wanted?

Five

I KISSED HIM BACK, and we made out like teenagers. I didn't fight the elation; I didn't fight my heart bursting with pure adoration and love.

We started undressing each other right there. I stopped and took Stu's hand, pulling his arm gently. He stood and followed me, stopping every few steps to make out some more.

In my bedroom, clothes dropped to the floor, and then we were both naked on my bed. This wasn't just sex; this was true lovemaking. Stu looked into my eyes the whole time, watching to make sure I was feeling just as good as he was. It went on for hours, both of us exploding more than once.

Our sweaty bodies wrapped together like two snakes twisted around each other. Then the anger hit. I pushed him off me and had my way with his body until it felt cheap, which didn't take long. Stu noticed what was happening and took back over so smoothly, like my anger never showed up. It was so beautiful. Once more we climaxed together.

Stu rolled into a position that allowed me to lay on my side, my smile mirroring his. He pushed a bit of hair from my face.

"How do you feel now?"

I closed my eyes, still smiling. "Like I just want to lay here in your arms and go to sleep."

I woke the next morning in the exact position I'd fallen asleep in for the first time in a long time. I looked at Stu's sleeping face and smiled before moving his arm to get up. I was happy and angry all at once. It was such a strange way to feel after such a wonderful night. I started the shower and got in once the water was the right temperature.

Stu woke while I was rinsing the conditioner from my hair and joined me. Last night's activities started all over again. I stopped it at kissing. My emotions weren't allowing me to enjoy the physical sensations now. Stopping was difficult; I hesitated and kept kissing Stu back. My conflict frustrated me, and I accidentally bit Stu's lip. If I couldn't effectively stop myself, my brain could.

"Oh! I'm so sorry!" I felt terrible.

Stu touched his lip, showed me blood on his fingers, and laughed. "You have a habit of making men bleed."

If you only knew the half of it.

I handed him some soap. "Wash it off, man. It's gonna sting no matter what you do."

We switched places, me pulling a towel off the shower door. "How are you gonna explain the fat lip?"

"I'll just tell people you punched me," he joked.

I rolled my eyes, wrapping the towel around my body, and got out.

It's Saturday, so I don't have to get to work, but I wasn't sure what Stu's schedule looked like. I dried off and wrapped a towel in my hair so I could finish my routine. I was putting clothes on when Stu turned the water off.

"Thanks, Brit."

"For what?"

"The towel you left on the door."

"I only did it so you wouldn't drip all over my floors." I laughed and tripped into my leggings, laughing harder.

"What's so funny?" Stu was rubbing his hair with the towel as he walked in. He laughed with me. "You're a mess."

"I know but you love me anyway."

"I do."

We stared at each other for an awkward minute. I broke the silence.

"What are your plans today?"

"I have to work at four."

"That's a weird shift. Don't you work twelves?"

"Normally, yeah. I took some overtime today for the football game."

"I forgot there was a game," I replied, the gears in my head turning.

"What are you thinking?"

"Maybe I'll go tailgate with the girls," I mused.

"Do they even like football?"

"Kristen, Shae, and…shit. I think just those two. Eh, cheaper for us that way."

"So, what lot will you be in? I can help keep you girls safe," Stu said, trying to sound tough.

"Hah! You know I'll have my Shield on me. I think we'll manage."

"You're so full of shit! You're gonna get drunk and then what? Can you defend yourself then?"

"Is that a challenge, Office Jones?"

"You went there? Really?"

I huffed. "Sorry. I didn't mean to sound like a dick. I've never been too drunk to fight back. Something about the flight-or-fight response sobers me up."

"That's the correct answer. I'm sorry too. I wasn't trying to get on your nerves."

Stu was dressed before I even finished hooking my bra. I guess cops are used to changing clothes fast. I knew he never went in wearing his uniform, preferring to change in the locker room. It was a safety concern. I could understand that. I always had a change of clothes, but for much different purposes.

Lately I was growing more and more frazzled and fraying at the edges. I could fly off and kill someone for a stupid reason; I felt that in my bones. I needed to get myself back together or stop the fraying somehow. I pulled a jersey over my head and noticed Stu watching me.

"What?"

"You're cute when you're lost in your thoughts." He smiled and walked over, kissed me on the cheek. "But I can't stand here watching you all day. I have to go grab my work stuff and get to headquarters."

"Be safe. Call you when I get there."

"Any idea which lot yet?"

"Hmm…what's the one kind of behind the stadium on Himes? That one."

"Lot 14. Got it." Stu kissed me before he left. I kissed back, hard again.

"Ouch." Stu grabbed his lip again.

I blushed. "Forgot. Sorry."

Stu let himself out, and I flopped my ass onto my bed, slumping over. Before I let myself feel much more, I grabbed my phone from the nightstand and texted Kristen and Shae. Then I tossed my phone to the side and slumped further.

My feelings were heavy. I don't recall a time I was this internally conflicted about anything more than how to kill someone or dispose of their body. This was all so new. And frustrating. My phone dinged, pulling me from the depths of mind fuck.

I'm down, came Kristen's reply.

Me too!

I typed back, *Cool, who's bringing what?*

The conversation continued for two more minutes with us deciding what we were taking, and they decided to meet here and either get a rideshare or I would drive.

Now that our plans were settled, I went downstairs to feed Minion and go pick up the provisions I'd agreed to. Minion stretched on the couch and eyed me like I'd forgotten about her in my night of bliss.

"Okay, fine. I did. But I'll give you extra treats tonight."

She purred and followed me to the kitchen. I filled her bowl and put it in her spot, then picked up my things and put sneakers on.

The volume on the Jeep's radio was loud. Now I knew how Stu knew I was home from picking up dinner. Was I deaf? Damn! I turned it down and could hear myself think again, so back up the volume went.

The parking lot wasn't quite as busy as I'd expected for a game day Saturday. There had to be something going on I didn't know about that caused people to just not be on the roads the past two days.

As for today's game, it wasn't really a game. It was a scrimmage between the Air Force and Army teams from MacDill. I won't pretend to understand how military football works. I heard someone say something about it being a charity game and members from each branch were playing for fun. Maybe we'd get tickets and go in. I still planned to tailgate like a champ. I have a table, two chairs, and tent. Kristen was bringing a small grill and Shae some extra chairs.

Kristen called and said she was coming early because she wanted to food shop together. I wanted to call Shae and ask her to join us, but it'd been so long since it was just Kristen and I, that I didn't bother. Besides, how hard is it to buy chips and dip?

I checked the weather and decided to change into jeans from the leggings I had on; it was supposed to rain. I put my Doc Martens by the door since they're waterproof and cute. Today was about fun and good people. Being practical is just part of who I am.

The doorbell couldn't have rung at a more perfect time. I opened the door to see Kristen's smiling face and hugged her.

"Hey! It's been a while," she greeted, hugging me.

"It has. So much and not so much going on," I replied, hugging her back. I gave the whatever shrug as I let her in.

"Like what? You know I'm not telling any of the others."

I wanted to tell her everything, including the slow unravel and almost being caught too many times, but I'd leave those bits out. Instead, I opened up about Stu. Of course, I had to perpetuate the lie that my career didn't quite allow for a relationship right now.

Kristen laughed before replying, "You're so full of shit!"

"Yeah, but I barely get to see you all lately. That's not the kind of life I want to live. I'd be more comfortable having the time to spend with those I love. It'll happen."

Kristen agreed.

"So, you're just going to, what? Let things happen?"

"What else am I supposed to do? We enjoy each other's company and don't want to stop hanging out. Maybe I'll clarify boundaries? Here's hoping that works."

We got into my Jeep and drove to Publix. There, we picked up snacks, drinks, hot dogs, and burgers. And beer and wine and soda. No tailgate is complete without the drinks. I was getting hungry just thinking about grilling. We checked out separately and got back to my house just in time to meet Shae.

I hopped down, waving to Shae.

"Since mine's already running, I'll drive."

"Cool," Shae said as she turned back toward her car.

Kristen hopped out of my Jeep and went over to help Shae, taking the chairs from her and loading them into the back before going to her car and pulling out the grill and propane bottles. Shae pulled out four paper grocery bags. Two were snack-filled, two were drink-filled. I laughed as I opened the back door, taking bags from Shae and placing them on the floor behind the passenger seat.

Kristen put the grill and propane into my Jeep and climbed into the passenger seat. Shae hopped in behind my seat, locking her car with the fob from her perch.

I pulled myself up and drove off, blasting hard rock on the way out to piss off the nosey old lady.

Six

TRAFFIC GETTING INTO THE lot wasn't as bad as it would be for a normal football game. We didn't even have to pay to park. Whatever. The game was for a good cause. I drove to where the attendant pointed and backed into a spot that allowed for me to open the rear door and pop the tent right there.

The three of us got out and pulled the tent into the grass where we wanted to situate it. The ground was flat and soft enough for the stakes. We amused ourselves struggling to fully set it up, and a drunk woman came over to offer her help. We looked at each other and shrugged "why not?"

What a show the four of us now were. I only wished I had a seat to watch it. We laughed so hard, making it that much harder to put the tent up. But we finally got it. To thank her for the help, we invited her to join us for food when it was ready. She thanked us, saying she had some but would love for us to go play cornhole with her and her friends. We agreed and thanked her again.

"I haven't played cornhole in forever," Shae said as we started unloading everything else from the back of the Jeep.

"I've never played," Kristen remarked, setting up the table.

"Shit. Don't look at me. I have no idea what's even happening right now," I joked.

Kristen pulled the table open, and together we unfolded the legs and set it up. The next ten minutes were a flurry of movement, each of us setting up chairs and food and the grill. The one thing we forgot to bring with us was a cooler. Oops. The people parked next to us let us put what we needed to in theirs, which was cool of them. In return, we shared our food and drinks. It was a *real* tailgate now. I put on some music in the Jeep and turned it up loud enough for us to dance to. We got our party on while we grilled and had a really great time.

We'd been there for about an hour before I text Stu.

Hey! Hungry?

We had plenty of food to share, and he'd need to eat at some point.

A few minutes later, I got a response. *Where are you?*

Lot 14, about 12 rows in on the right side. Call when you get here, and I'll walk out to meet you.

Okay.

It seemed abrupt, or maybe I was overanalyzing, I couldn't tell. But I decided I might try to figure it out when he got here. His in-person demeanor would be the tell of how he was reacting to our romp last night.

My phone rang eight minutes later.

"I'm here. Where are you?" Stu asked before I could properly answer.

"You sound exhausted," I poked as I started walking out to the drive that connected the entire lot with Himes Ave.

"I am, thanks to you." I could hear a smile on the other end.

"You helped me stay awake, so I figured it only fair."

I'd barely gotten three rows down when I was attacked from my left. I dropped my phone and tried to swing but found my arms pinned to my sides.

Stu hugged me so tight.

"Can't…breathe…"

He released me. "I didn't mean to get you that tight. Sorry."

After catching my breath. I hugged him back.

I looked into his eyes, seeing very clearly that he was not mad at me in any way. I kissed his cheek and turned to walk back to our area. Stu followed.

"How's it going so far?" I asked, picking my phone up.

"Slow. It's weird."

"Yeah, it is. Anything going on at this stadium is usually pretty busy. Any amusement, at least?"

"A little, mostly kids and already trashed adults. Some elderly people have been extra sassy." He blushed as he said that last bit.

"Did some old lady slap your ass again?"

"Yes."

I started cracking up just as we reached the tent and revelers.

"What's so funny?" Shae asked as she spun to greet us.

"Old ladies slapping Stu's ass," I replied and snorted. "Stu, what do you want to drink?"

"You pick."

I grabbed a Coke Zero and handed it to him.

"Thanks." He pulled the tab to open the can and took a deep drink.

I plated a cheeseburger and two hot dogs and handed them to him. He nodded his thanks and drained his soda. I grabbed him another and a beer for myself.

"Anyone want anything while I'm over here?"

The neighbors shook their heads. "No, thanks."

"I'll take a beer," Kristen said.

I looked at Shae. "Anything?"

She raised her right hand; in it was a beer.

"Okay then."

I tossed Kristen a beer and walked back to our chairs. I chose the one next to me for Stu and placed the can inside the built-in cup holder. Stu was over at the table, adding onions and mustard to his hot dogs.

He spotted me and the empty chair as soon as he turned around. He came and sat, eating a hot dog on the short walk.

"I can't stay long. I think I have, like, thirty or so minutes."

"Why not an hour?"

"It's an OT shift, so I decided to split the hour." He winked at me.

"I don't know what you think we can do in such a short amount of time."

We all laughed.

"Ass. I meant to make sure you get out of here okay. I see you drove." He took a bite of his burger, nodded at my Jeep, then continued talking, "I'll follow you home. Kinda had a feeling you'd drive anyway."

"You are nothing if not observant," I commented.

Shae and Kristen looked at each other, expressions saying it all.

Stu blew off the sarcasm in my tone, continuing to eat his food. I emptied my beer and stood for another. I waved my bottle, everyone knowing I was asking if they wanted any-thing. Kristen stood, shaking her head, and grabbed a plate off the table. Shae followed her. I shrugged and grabbed myself and Stu another drink each.

Stu took the can offered and nodded his thanks as he cleared his plate. With Kristen and Shae now seated and hap-pily munching, I walked over to the table. I grabbed a plate and put two cheeseburgers and one bun-less hot dog on it. I'm not a fan of hot dog buns; they're usually too dry. They made good weapons if you let them sit out all day, though. I smirked as that thought slipped away while I added onions and mayo to my burgers.

On my way back to my chair, I munched on the hot dog, for once not being facetious about it by gesturing and making eye contact with Stu. I was hungry. I did notice Stu watching me as I sat down but chose to ignore it. I may have initiated last night, but I also made my feelings about a relationship more than clear. The ones people were allowed to know about anyway.

Finishing his drink, Stu stood and looked at me. I checked my watch; it was that time. I got up, placing my plate on my seat, and started to walk with him. He said "bye" to the girls and led the way. I followed, catching Kristen's expression from the corner of my eye; the look of "just fucking date the guy" clear as day. I shook my head and picked up my pace.

"Let me know when you're leaving, please?"

"Why? So you can be the arresting officer?" I joked.

"So I can follow you, duh," he replied. "Did you forget I said that?"

"I did. Sorry."

"Brit, are you okay?"

'Yeah. I'm good. Just conflicted. No biggie." I was now lying to myself too.

Stu turned and hugged me. I hugged back, fighting the anger.

"You're too good to me, Stu."

"I adore you, Brit." He kissed my cheek and went back to work, leaving me alone with my thoughts and anger.

I stood there and watched him leave until he was a smaller person, finally disappearing after turning the corner. A single tear of frustration rolled down my cheek.

The Miami blood guy had a partner. Or was it ultimately two? Doesn't matter; they existed was all that mattered.

But they sorta helped put him back on the cops' radar. Well, that was the show. In the books he didn't have a partner and…well, shit. Could I even consider a partner? Could I consider that Stu could accept what I am? Fuck.

I walked back to my friends and tossed the thoughts aside in favor of beer and food. I'd mull over these things—and more—when I could have a conversation with myself. For now, I intended to enjoy my time with friends.

We drank, ate, and drank some more. We played cornhole with the lady who helped us pop the tent, then we decided to go watch the game a bit. The neighbor who was letting us use cooler space stopped us.

"We have a TV and satellite; we can stay here and watch the game," he told us.

"Really? That's awesome of you," Shae said to him, then looked from me to Kristen. "Want to stay here? We can finish our food in comfort."

She had a point, but I still wanted to do something in support of whatever charity the game was benefiting.

"Do you know what charity they're playing for?" I asked the neighbor.

"I do! It's for military families who are taking care of loved ones who can't take care of themselves due to something that happened while they were in the service. Let me go see if my wife has the name. It's easier that way. And I don't want to fuck up telling you what they do. Hang on, I think she's got a brochure or something." His voice trailed as he walked away.

Kristen tapped my shoulder. "What are you doing?"

"I want to donate or something. Maybe they'll have a raffle going on or stuff to buy that helps them out, you know?"

Kristen nodded her agreement, and Shae joined in too. It was now official that they would also be supporting the charity.

Our neighbor returned, handing me the brochure. "She said to keep it. Apparently, she took a picture *and* has already gotten raffle tickets."

"Sweet! Thanks! Now to find raffle tickets for us," I said, the girls again nodding.

We walked back to our tent, me flipping through the brochure. There was a bit about raffle tickets being sold by people walking around each lot. It also said something about them wearing distinct t-shirts. Further, it noted a number to text if it got close to halftime and we still wanted to buy tickets for the drawing.

I told the girls what it said, and Shae decided to text the number, laughing at me and how easily I seemed to be forgetting things lately. I raised my beer in a mock toast and laughed. She wasn't wrong, though. I was forgetting more than I usually did. I'd get back on track soon. Forgetting things was just another thing added to the list of shit that was getting on my nerves; read "Britney's Unraveling."

The kids selling the raffle tickets came around, and we each bought some. Between the three of us, I think we'd gotten around thirty or forty. They thanked us, wished us luck, and moved on. Helping always felt good, no matter how I did it. I didn't care if I won. In my mind, I already did by getting the tickets. I made a mental note to look further into monthly donations to this group and others like it.

The neighbor called over to us that kickoff was in two minutes. We put our tickets in our pockets and walked over to his camper, pausing to grab beers for us and them. We handed them the beers and clinked in toast.

Then we heard a rumble and the sky opened up.

Seven

THE RAIN POUNDED us. We tried to run back under my tent for cover, but it stopped as quick as it started. Florida weather was weird like that. The entire spring season, it would rain for about forty-five minutes at almost the same time every day. I remember one year; it was so predictable that you could set your watch by it. It got more unpredictable as the years went on, with some not having much rain at all. Climate change is an actual thing.

Even though I knew it was supposed to rain, I didn't bring any towels—no one did. I did, however, have contractor bags. We'd have to sit on those on the way back to my house.

Shae, being Shae, decided to try shaking off like a dog. She'd had a bit to drink and slipped, landing on her ass on the hard ground. It didn't rain long enough to soak in. We all burst into hysterical laughter. Even Shae laughed as she struggled to get back up. Kristen reached a hand out for Shae to grab onto. We were still laughing, and Kristen lost her grip, stumbling but regaining her footing quickly. She helped Shae up and grabbed a bottle of wine.

"This is well deserved," she said, looking at the bottle as a reward.

The neighbors handed out red plastic cups while Kristen got the bottle open. Even with the brief downpour, we had a magnificent time and even met some really cool people. The group of us drank the first bottle of wine in less than five minutes. I think that's a new record that us ladies will have to beat now.

Kickoff wasn't delayed, and the satellite worked well. The game started off like any other football game, with the receiving team driving hard. The defenders were brutal. I had a feeling this game would injure quite a few people. I was glad we weren't in the stands; from what I could see on the TV, spectators were even more rowdy than the players

By the end of the first quarter, I was bored. I grabbed a beer and joined the drunk lady and her friends for another game of cornhole. That game took up less than seven minutes. I thanked them for letting me play again and went back to my friends.

"Hey. When do y'all want to leave?" I asked them.

Kristen answered first. "You drove so we follow your lead."

"Bad answer," I replied with a smirk.

"Fine. How about after the drawing?" Shae suggested.

Kristen and I looked at each other and nodded.

"Sounds good to me," I said.

"Cool. So we'll start packing as soon as we finish our beers," Kristen offered.

We all smiled, saluted, and chugged.

Shae rubbed her ass as we packed up, complaining that she'd have a nasty bruise by tomorrow.

"That's what happens when you like it rough," I joked.

Shae laughed so hard she snorted. "What was that about you dominating the valet kid?" she shot back.

Did I tell her about him? I couldn't remember. Another mental note.

We kept chatting and laughing as we finished packing and loading up. The process had gone much quicker than the unload and setup did. Wasn't that the way, though? The memory of packing things for the branch office and setting up new workstations flashed in my mind. I found myself unexpectedly missing Julie even more.

I shook the thoughts away and thanked the neighbor for being so cool. We shook hands, and I gave him one of my cards.

"We'll do this again," he said and smiled.

I nodded and got into my Jeep. The girls were already buckled in, waiting for me.

"Shit. Stu wants me to call him," I said, pulling my phone out of my pocket.

I opened the phone app and swiped to dial. It rang once before Stu answered.

"I'll be right there," he said. "I'm at the corner of Himes and MLK but I have to get the car. Meet me at the end of the drive in three minutes."

"Got it."

I heard Stu talking to whoever he was working with, then the line went dead.

"Okay, ladies, we've got a whole two-and-a-half minutes before I can pull out of this spot," I joked.

"Like my seven-point-two-minute arrival times?" Kristen said.

"Exactly!"

Shae looked confused. Kristen and I just laughed again. We'd tell Shae. Maybe.

Kristen turned the radio on and found a song that I hate. She loved it, so she turned it up in jest. "Happy" by Pharrell makes me anything but.

"What about the raffle tickets? Do we need to be here to win?" Shae asked.

"Shit. Let me see if the game's being broadcast," I replied, grateful for a second reason to turn that garbage off.

Then I changed the setting to one of the satellite channels that broadcasts the game and shifted to pull my raffle tickets out of my pocket. The girls wrangled their tickets from pockets too. The broadcast had switched from analytics to halftime. We heard kids pulling the numbers and adults reading them into the microphone. We checked, but none of us won.

"Dammit. I never win anything," Shae complained.

"Um, but you did win," I shot back.

"What did I win?"

"You won the friend lottery, dummy. With friends like us, you don't need others!"

She and Kristen cackled with glee. I giggled and pulled out of the spot. Kristen tried searching the channels for something we could all dance to, but there wasn't anything. So she left a rock station playing and started talking to Shae.

I pulled up to the exit and saw Stu in his patrol car waiting for us. He motioned for me to pull out, and I shook my head. He made a face, then pointed to the officer directing traffic. I looked left and saw him waving me on. I hadn't seen him when I first pulled up, so I shrugged and drove out.

The drive home felt like it took longer than usual, but in reality, it didn't. I guessed it was because I wasn't dancing around. Or maybe it was because I was being followed by a patrol car.

At a red light a few blocks from my house, I turned to Kristen and Shae.

"You guys gonna hang for a bit or no?"

Shae made a noise, then said, "Nah. I'm going home. I think a nap is in order."

The light changed while she was talking, so I kept driving.

"I'll stay for a bit," Kristen replied. "My parents are in town, so they have the kid."

"Ohhhh shit! Party time!"

We all laughed as I pulled into my driveway and parked. Shae got out first, went to the back door, and opened it. Kristen and I hopped down from our seats and joined Shae, unloading the table, tent, and chairs. With all that propped up against the back of my Jeep, I went to the keypad for the garage and entered the numbers to open it. Kristen was first to put the table inside, followed by Shae with my chairs. I grabbed the tent and stored it. Then Kristen helped Shae load her chairs in her car.

I walked over to Shae and hugged her. "Thanks for coming with us!"

"Thanks for inviting me! It was fun. We should do it again," she agreed.

You must be under the impression you're going to live much longer…

"Definitely."

"Oh yeah," said Kristen.

Shae got in her car, waved, and drove away.

Kristen looked at me funny. "I feel like something's off with her."

"You too?" I agreed. I already knew what she was hiding. But I suspected there was more to her story than she told me.

We grabbed the remaining food and drinks and carried them into the house. For once, Minion didn't scream at my arrival. Instead, she glared at us like we interrupted her or something. She was sprawled out on the couch; we definitely interrupted. We laughed at her on our way into the kitchen.

Kirsten set her bag on the counter and started unpacking. I joined her, and we had everything put away in less than three minutes. Then she turned from the fridge, bottle of wine in hand. I pulled two glasses down, and Kristen poured. We clinked and took our glasses—and the bottle—into the living room.

I slid Minion from her comfort, drawing more irritation from such a compact ball of fur. We sat and turned Netflix on for our favorite shared pastime: watching awful b-horror movies. We gravitated to a shark flick featuring holographic sharks living in the sand.

We laughed so hard, we both exhaled wine through our noses. It did *not* feel good, more like fire. We laughed even harder, of course, at ourselves. And we were relatively sober. We just appreciated terrible movies for what they really were: horror comedy.

When the movie ended, Kristen checked the time on her phone. "Shit. I should go. I'm sure my parents are having a wonderful time, but it's child bedtime at nine, and I gotta feed her."

I stood up with her. "It's all good. I'm glad we had the chance to do this. When she's old enough, we'll get her into these awesome movies," I said and laughed.

I walked her to the door and hugged her. After she left, I locked the door. This neighborhood might be safe enough, but I also know safety is nothing more than an illusion. Besides, with killers like me on the loose, how safe is safe?

I needed to not think about Stu, so I plopped back down on the couch for another bad movie. Then my phone dinged.

Hey! How are you? It was Devin.

Oh, hey! I'm good. You?

Good. So I'm off early tonight and was thinking…

Was thinking? Good, don't hurt yourself.

Wow…

That was harsh, wasn't it? What I meant was to stop thinking. I'm not in the mood.

Oh.

I didn't bother to respond and set my phone back on the table. Then it started ringing. I answered without paying attention to the name on the Caller ID.

"Was I not bitchy enough? What the fuck do you want?"

"Uh, Brit…you good?" Stu asked.

My face turned red. "Oh wow. I'm so sorry. I thought you were someone else."

"It's cool." He chuckled. "I was actually calling to apologize."

"For what?"

"I had to break off from following you home while we were still on Dale Mabry."

"I didn't notice. Us girls were chatting, and I didn't even think to look in the mirror. I was too busy making sure I stayed the speed limit."

Now Stu laughed. "Does it take that much concentration?"

"Yes. Yes it does," I said, my tone serious.

"You crack me up, Brit."

"I try, I guess. Well, you're forgiven."

"Thanks. So what are your plans tonight? I'm done with work…"

I felt like shit for what was about to come out of my mouth. "Stu, I don't think we should…"

"I know, but…I want to so bad."

"If I can't give you what you deserve right now, what makes you think dinner together would make it any better?"

"I don't think that. I just want to spend time with you. Maybe I hope to change your mind…"

"Stu, my dear, sweet Stu. I adore you with all my heart. Which is why I can't say yes. It's not fair to either of us. As cliché as it is, I don't want to hurt you."

"And I thank you for that, but Brit, come on. I thought we agreed we could still be friends until whatever happens, happens?"

"We did. But we also agreed that we'd cut back on how much time we spent together."

Stu sighed. "We did." He sighed again, heavier this time. "Okay. I love you, Brit. Glad you're home safe."

"I love you too, Stu."

We hung up, and I slumped back on the couch. Minion came over to me and jumped onto my lap. I guess she knew how shitty I felt.

I went back to watching mind-numbingly stupid movies in an effort to distract myself. This one was something about piranha eating people. I'd seen it before and liked it. But now I couldn't get into it. So, I picked up my phone and started playing one of those bubble pop games, with the movie as background noise.

The doorbell rang as the movie ended.

Eight

I CONTEMPLATED ANSWERING FOR a full thirty seconds. The bell sounded again, and I sighed and looked at Minion before I stood to get it. I opened the door, made one of my famous facial expressions, and walked back to the couch, leaving the door open for Stu to walk in.

He spoke as he closed it. "I shouldn't be here, I know. But I don't care. I wanted to hug you. I'll leave after that."

I eyed him and plopped back onto the couch.

"Stay. We'll eat dinner soon. I'll ignore the elevated creeper status of you calling me from outside my house," I said, flipping through more b-horror movies.

Stu came to sit next to me. "Okay then. Thanks."

I appreciated that he was here. Hell, I even appreciated the near stalking. I just didn't want to admit it to him. I put my head on his shoulder and enjoyed the fact that he refused to listen to reason. Could I keep him around and still be able to kill others without him knowing?

I forced that thought out of my mind and sat up. There wasn't anything I wanted to watch right now.

"Any ideas for dinner?" I asked as I turned my entire body to face him.

"No. Like I said, I just wanted a hug and was gonna leave after that."

"Well, Stu Jones, you're stuck with me now." I smirked at him. I wasn't sure if I meant just for the night or forever.

"You won't hear me complain."

I stood and went to the kitchen to retrieve my stash of paper menus from local food joints. There was everything from pizza to Chinese, Mexican to Peruvian. It was a bit overwhelming. I settled on my fallback of pizza. Stu agreed. It was greasy, cheesy goodness that no one could say no to.

"I'm not so picky about toppings, so you can choose. Well, as long as it's not anchovies. And if you add pineapple, no red sauce."

Stu's mouth fell open. "I don't know if we can be friends now."

"I'm sorry, say that again?" My tone revealed venom, verging on outright anger. I stared at him, waiting for an answer.

"You put pineapple on pizza."

"Only with BBQ sauce, NOT red sauce. What the fuck, man? We're really gonna not be friends over that?"

Stu laughed. "Of course not. Pineapple with red sauce is gross. I've never had it with BBQ, though. Well, not on pizza."

"You've never had a Papa John's Hawaiian BBQ Chicken pizza before?"

"Um, no?"

"Okay, that's dinner. We can order fries elsewhere since they don't have them."

I picked up my phone and asked Google to call the closest location. I was being too lazy to look up the number myself. Besides, technology wasn't my best friend, but it did a good enough job making my life easier.

I felt better knowing Stu was joking, but damn. My fucking anxiety would kill me before anything else could.

As I ordered the pizza, Stu called and ordered the fries.

"Hang on a sec," he said into the phone, then looked at me and said, "I'll go pick it up."

I nodded. "Oh, sorry. Can we change it to pickup, please? Yeah, my friend's gonna come get it…Stu is his name, Stu Jones. Okay, so I can pay now?"

We both finished our conversations, and Stu looked at me funny.

"What?"

"I would've gotten that."

"Don't be silly. It's a pizza, for shit's sake."

"How long did they say?"

"Thirty minutes."

"Okay, I'll leave now then. The fries will be done first, then I'll grab the pizza and be back. Sound good?"

"Sure. Any movie preference?"

"Nah. You pick." Stu kissed me on the cheek and left.

I put the menus away and came back to find something for us to watch.

It felt like ten minutes had gone by when Stu got back. In reality, it was closer to thirty. He walked into the house and straight to the kitchen. I stood to follow, but he gave me another weird look. I followed anyway.

"Absolutely not, Stewart!" I admonished as I walked in. "You are not doing what I think you are."

He laughed as he took plates from the cabinet. "I have no idea what you're talking about."

"And you can stop with the weird looks too." I spoke into the refrigerator, but he heard me. I took out a couple beers, carrying them and my pizza.

"Fine. Whatever you say, Brit. You're the boss." His tone was lighthearted, but I was still on edge.

What was happening to me? Was it really anxiety? Was it control issues? I didn't really want to talk to Ben about this anymore and talking to the girls or Stu could be the shittiest idea ever. I wanted to tell someone what I am. That someone was Stu. FUCK!

We put all the fries on one plate and had separate plates for our slices. Stu held his plate to his nose and sniffed. "Smells good."

"You may just fall in love with it," I joked, walking back to the couch.

Stu grinned as he came over, carrying his pizza and the fries. We set the coffee table up like it was a dinner table and clinked bottles.

"To us," Stu said.

"Yes, to you learning how to stalk me," I giggled and took a swig, then pressed play on the remote.

The movie was one neither of us had seen but wanted to. Something about cannibals and it was released in 1985.

We didn't make the full hour and thirty-seven minutes; I think we made it to forty minutes. The fact that it was so old, combined with the found footage vibe, put me off and my face started its usual lack of discretion. I think I started making noises of boredom, too, because Stu looked at me like I'd lost my mind.

"What are you doing over there?"

"Huh? What do you mean?"

"Brit, you're making noises like a hog, and your facial expressions are running amok."

I laughed. "Amok, huh? Well, this movie is boring. That noise is one I make when I'm annoyed and bored at the same time. If you wanna be with me, you have to deal with it." I smirked and poked his leg.

"You're gonna have to do more than that to chase me away," he replied, leaning over and pecking me on the lips.

The movie played while we made out like teenagers whose parents left us alone for the first time. And, in truth, that's what being with him felt like. Every single time. I wondered if those feelings would pass and I'd grow bored of him like I did the movie. I pushed that thought aside in favor of enjoying our make-out session.

When I we came up for air, my face started again.

"What's wrong?" Stu asked, looking confused.

"Nothing. Why?" I was so full of it. I was sure I could've started a new landfill.

"Your face says otherwise."

"Sorry. I am feeling pretty torn."

"About?"

"Us. But I've *been* feeling this way, and you've known that."

Stu nodded. "I'm sorry. I shouldn't have come over. Want me to go?"

My eyes misted.

Nine

STU PICKED UP THE empty plates. I put a hand on his arm to stop him. He looked at me, his expression saying more than words ever could.

"Please—"

"I'm not mad. Promise." I struggled to smile.

He walked to the door, pausing before opening it. He started to turn around but stopped and walked out.

I fell backward into the couch and cried. Minion snuck into the mess that was me and cuddled me in an effort to console me. My heart hurt, something I never thought possible. Yet here it was, happening right now, and the only thing I could do to stop it was…No. I didn't want to stop seeing Stu at all. But I knew we couldn't date. Could we? If we tried and he found out, would it get real bad real fast? Or would he be accepting of his serial killer girlfriend? I wanted to find out as much as I didn't.

I sniffed one last time and forced myself off the couch to put the dirty dishes in the sink. I put the remaining pizza in the fridge and took out a bottle of wine. As I pulled a glass down, I contemplated just sticking a straw in the bottle, but didn't have one long enough. So, I settled on drinking from a glass like the human that I am.

Back on the couch, Minion looked at me sleepily.

"I know, but I'm not," I said to her, hoping it didn't qualify as crazy cat lady.

I drained my glass before finding something else to put on then went back into the kitchen. When I came back to the couch this time, I was armed. I had the bottle I'd just opened and another ready to go, opener dangling from my pinkie. I poured more wine and plopped back down, convinced I'd have a hangover tomorrow morning. Not that I cared.

I surfed some more, finally choosing *Reservoir Dogs*. That movie always took my mind off things.

By the time it was over, both bottles of wine were empty, and I couldn't stand up straight. Fearing I'd drop the glass, I left it on the table and stumbled my way upstairs and to bed.

The sun woke me up the next morning. I rolled over thinking about blackout curtains and almost squished Minion, not knowing she was there. I reached a hand down and pet her—my way of apologizing—my eyes still closed.

I didn't care what time it was; I just wanted to lie there forever. I felt awful. Not hangover awful. Heart awful. I wondered if Stu and I would ever talk again. But I was being dramatic. He'd call or text or even stop by. Just not today.

I managed to fall back to sleep for another two hours. I reached for my phone to check the time, but it wasn't on my nightstand. Not sure if I cared that it likely had half the battery left, I got out of bed and brushed my teeth. It was hard but forcing myself to keep as normal a routine as possible was important. If I couldn't, I'd fall apart entirely. Routines helped me stay focused, Sunday or not.

When I got downstairs, I started the coffee maker and searched for my phone. I found it on the coffee table, lighting up like the Fourth of July. So many missed texts from Shae, Kristen, and Danielle. I responded to Danielle's first.

Left my phone downstairs last night. Sorry. Still on for lunch this week?

Yes! Any place you want to go?

No. You choose.

Mexican it is.

I giggled out loud. Danielle adored Mexican food as much as I adored wine.

Just let me know which place and time and I'll be there.

OK.

I responded to Shae and Kristen on my walk back to the coffee maker. It may not have been finished brewing, but that didn't mean I couldn't pour a cup anyway. I sipped the blackness in and let out the pain. Then my phone beeped and showed a low-battery warning. I set the mug on the counter and found the spare charger I kept in here for days like this, and plugged the phone in. Then I opened the patio door, choosing to sit outside, until I felt the thick, nasty air, and slammed the door closed.

"Ugh! Gross!" I shivered at how sticky my skin was.

I refilled my cup and called Minion for her breakfast. She came tearing in as I filled her bowl and set it down in front of her. Then I went back upstairs to shower the gross away, annoyed that I wouldn't be jogging outside.

"It just *has* to be that yuck outside, right? The one day I really need to rid myself of negative energy," I complained to myself as I pulled out gym clothes to put on. I was determined to get some kind of physical, self-inflicted beat-down in.

I still had a membership for that gym where I found Brody, so that's where I went. I finished my thirty minutes on the treadmill and, as I stepped down to get a cleaning wipe, smacked right into Stu.

"Oh shit, my bad," I said as I looked up at him.

"No prob-lem," he stuttered when he realized it was me who'd run into him.

We both felt awkward and it showed on our faces.

"I'd ask what you're doing here, but I get the feeling your reason is the same as mine," I said, painting on a pained smile.

"It's super nasty outside, so yeah, I guess you're right. Cops get a good discount here too. And it's got more equipment than ours at headquarters does," he said, clearly uncomfortable about talking to me right now.

"Stu, I-I'm sorry about last night." I looked at the floor for a minute, unable to hold his gaze.

"So am I." His face turned pink and his eyes welled up. Mine did just looking back at him.

"I, uh, I gotta go," he stammered and trotted off toward the Smith Machine. I watched him, feeling my heart sink. This was unquestionably the worst pain I'd ever felt. I was positive this was why I never let any man this close before. Any human for that matter.

I wanted to scream. At Stu. At myself. At nothing. Instead I grabbed a couple cleaning wipes and vigorously wiped down the treadmill I'd just been on. It was all I could do to stop anger and truth from coming out of my mouth at Stu. I got mean when I was angry, and Stu didn't deserve for me to be mean to him. And he deserved the truth, but I couldn't tell him. Not here, and not now.

I stomped to the locker room to rinse my face off, hoping it might help a little. All that accomplished, though, was to rinse off the sweat. It was still better than nothing.

I walked out of the gym still angry and frustrated, though I seemed to hide it well. People walking in smiled and nodded at me, something they didn't do when they could see the anger. That made me feel significantly better. Maybe I was already getting back to myself.

The frustration lingered until I got home. I caved and texted Ben before getting another shower.

I need to see you.

Then I hit send.

The hot water felt wonderful. I let it rinse the sticky away and open my pores like a sauna. I took a long time washing my body and hair. This shower was the first peace I'd had all day. It was more relaxing than my jog on the treadmill. My phone dinged while I rinsed conditioner out of my hair. And, for once, I didn't rush to respond.

I shut the shower off when the water turned lukewarm. The bathroom was covered in a dense fog, so I cracked the window open and flipped the switch for the fan. Then I grabbed my phone and wiped the screen off. The message was from Ben.

What's up?

The feelings are getting worse. Please help.

I set the phone down again and dried myself off. I was continuing to feel better, bit by bit, but I was nowhere near where I wanted to be.

Maybe getting together with Shae would help if I couldn't see Ben today. She did say she had more she wanted to tell me; I wanted to figure out *why* I wanted to kill her. And how. I could start my KKD plan once I had a better understanding of the why—my reason for killing her.

The weirdest part was that I knew I'd kill her, but not the why. Between my killer instincts avoiding logic and my heart pain, I could see the walls I carefully constructed starting to crumble. My phone dinged again, yanking me from my contemplations.

Are you free in an hour?

I am.

Okay, meet me at my office.

Thanks, Ben.

I let my thoughts wander back to Shae. Going back through my time alone with her, I remembered being buzzed and telling her about Devin. I think I even offered to see if he had any single friends to introduce her to. She'd laughed at me, saying something about not being ready and making a joke about gaining another stalker.

Such a shame she didn't know she already had one. I smiled and finished getting ready for my appointment.

Ten

I WAS GLAD I'D left the house so early because I hit some serious traffic on my way to Ben's office. Sundays were always shit for traffic, but that's the norm for Tampa. Crowded roads were the signature of the area. Not the sugar sand beaches you'd see in a travel ad. Half the people on the roads weren't even Floridians; they were snowbirds.

I parked outside of Ben's office and took a deep breath. What, exactly, was I going to say? I didn't even think about that on the drive here. I was too pissed off at traffic. I sat there trying to gather my thoughts. I didn't bother to shut the Jeep off because I needed the air conditioning. I checked the clock on the radio screen and saw I still had a few minutes to work out what I was going to tell Ben. And I used every last bit I could to make sure I'd rehearsed a couple lines.

I opened the door and hopped down. I straightened myself out—physically and mentally—then walked to the door, locking my Jeep on the walk. Safety was the one illusion I was always good at seeing through. Or maybe I was just paranoid. I chose to believe the former as I greeted Ben.

"Hey! Thanks so much for seeing me today."

The waiting area wasn't white or gray like a typical doctor's office. It was a beautiful shade of lilac—or maybe it was lavender, I never understood the difference. The walls were decorated with degrees and awards in frames, making me feel a sense of calm. There was a gray couch against one wall and a small black table in the corner to the right of it. On the table stood one of those oil or wax burner things. It smelled like lemon and mint. It was soothing. The feel of the office was part of why I'd chosen Ben as my shrink.

Ben smiled and stood from the chair he was sitting in. "If I can help you, you know I will," he said, "but don't get used to me working on a Sunday."

I laughed. "Don't worry, I don't even like being here on a Sunday."

I followed him into his office and sat on a chair across from his. It was the same gray as the couch in the waiting area. It looked to have the same material and felt cushy. I think he'd gotten new furniture since the last time I was here.

"Are you comfortable with me leaving the door open?" he asked before he sat.

"Sure. I doubt anyone would come in."

He nodded. "So, tell me what's going on."

I took a deep breath and let fly. "Remember those feelings I said I fell into? Yeah…"

For the next twenty-five minutes, I told Ben everything that had gone on since the last time we talked. I told him everything—shy of being a killer. I wanted to tell him that, too, but I wanted to tell Stu more, so I chose to keep it secret until I couldn't anymore. I *knew* the words would come out. Like that episode of *Dexter* where he told the shrink he was a killer before killing him. That would be me. It was simply a question of when.

"Britney, your feelings are perfectly normal."

"Not for me. I've worked so hard to not feel things like love. Frustration and anger are normal."

"So, you're afraid of love. Also normal."

"I am NOT! If I was, do you think I'd still be okay hanging out with Stu? I'm just saying now isn't the time. And I'm afraid to hurt Stu. I'm an asshole, if you couldn't tell."

Ben chuckled. "Oh, I can tell. Britney, what I want you to do, right now, is role play. Talk to me like I'm Stu."

"Nope," I said, shaking my head. "I don't role play except…well, you get it. Besides, there are things I want to tell him that I can't tell you." I sounded like a teenager; talking to one parent about them being easier to talk to than the other. I was glad I wasn't actually like that when I was a teenager; I could talk to both of my parents.

"Then you need a plan. Something to help you be more forthcoming with Stu."

"Why? Why do I need to plan what I'm saying? Why not that—what do you call it?—stream of consciousness?"

"Because you're keeping something from me and without knowing what that is, I can't help you clear your brain enough to have a rational conversation with Stu."

I sat there silent for a few minutes, thinking about that.

"Let me get this straight. Because I'm not forthcoming with *you*, I'm incapable of it with Stu?"

"That's not what I meant."

"Please, tell me what you *do* mean." I didn't bother trying to hide the irritation in my voice.

"Brit, come on," Ben pleaded.

"No, Ben. What are you trying to say? That I'm losing it? I know that! That's why I'm here! Be straight with me." I leaned forward as I spoke, my eyes feeling like they would leave my face and tear Ben to pieces.

Ben sucked in a sharp breath, unfazed by the murderous look in my eyes.. "You implicitly trust me. For you to be hiding anything isn't good. Worse since you'd rather tell a cop than your therapist. Do you know how bad that sounds?"

I sat back in my chair, clasped my hands, and rested my chin on my thumbs. I watched Ben for what felt like a long time. Then I put my hands on the arms of the chair and stood.

"Bill me," I said and walked out.

I was mad, and I knew I shouldn't be. Ben was my therapist; he was *supposed* to say things like that to me. That's the whole point of a therapist-patient relationship. I unlocked my Jeep and swung the door open so hard it swung back at me, hitting me in the ribs.

"FUCK!" I screamed as I clutched my left side.

I took a few steadying breaths, cursed some more under my breath, and bit down on the pain as I climbed up into the driver's seat. I started the engine and turned the radio up. I needed to hear something violent, so I turned on "Bleeding Mascara" by Atreyu and drove away.

Look how pretty she is when she falls down…

Have I fallen down?

Now there's no beauty in bleeding mascara…

But there is beauty in it.

Her lips are quivering like a withering rose…

I am not a withering rose!

I banged on the steering wheel, angrier now than I was earlier. How was this possible? First, Ben called me out. Now, a song is calling me out? What was happening? I felt so attacked by the two biggest things I entrusted my mind—and sanity—to.

I got home and parked in the garage. People knew I parked in there, but sometimes not seeing the Jeep in the driveway was enough to stop people from random visits. I hated those anyway. I preferred if they called first. Julie and Stu were the exceptions, but I didn't think Stu would be stopping in unannounced for a while.

In the house, I took my shoes off and put them where they belonged by the front door. Then I went upstairs to shower again. I was over this day and wanted my pajamas and Chinese delivery. I think Minion could tell I was in a nasty mood because she didn't even lift a paw to follow me.

I turned the water to the hottest my skin could handle in the hopes of the anger washing out. The only thing that accomplished was burning my scalp, which made my mood worse. I turned the water off and broke down, sitting down in the shower, knees to chest, and cried. I cried until my skin got cold and started to dry.

"Dammit, Britney. Stop this feeling bullshit and get back to yourself." I wiped my eyes but didn't feel the determination I heard in my voice. I stood, dried off, and put my pajamas on.

"Fine. Just tonight. Tomorrow you go back to being you."

I felt a bit better after letting the feelings out, so I agreed with myself about getting back to "normal" tomorrow. Before I went back downstairs, though, I stood in front of my full-length mirror and watched myself. I didn't notice anything unusual, so I shrugged and went to the one place I knew I could be without feeling judged: the safe in my closet.

I twisted the dial, getting the combination right, and opened the door. The tools and supplies inside called to me, begging for release, screaming for playtime. The sight made me think more about the prospect of having a dedicated kill knife.

Soon. I promise. I need to play as much as you do.

I closed the door, turned the dial to lock it, and went downstairs. I turned the TV on and pulled my phone from my pocket to order dinner. When the order showed confirmed, I grabbed the remote and surfed. I didn't quite know what I wanted to watch, so I flipped through until something jumped out at me. That something was an urban fantasy spin-off show. I had originally started watching it hoping to see specific characters. When that didn't happen, I kept watching anyway; the show had done its job and sucked me in. I still hoped to see the main character's father, but that was the equivalent of "wish in one hand and shit in the other."

I was so absorbed, I barely heard the doorbell when my dinner arrived.

"Be right there!" I called, waiting for a break in the dialogue to hit the pause button. When the witch twin stopped threatening her father and sister three seconds later, I paused it.

I opened the door and uttered something that sounded like a squeal.

"Devin! Hi! What are you doing here?"

He held up a paper bag and didn't say a word. I took the bag, nodded, and closed the door. I have been real dick to him, but that didn't mean he couldn't be professional. I opened the delivery app back up to check that I'd tipped well enough. Satisfied I did, I put my phone back in my pocket and sat down to eat. I emptied the bag onto the table and stared at the assortment, egg rolls, fried dumplings, Mongolian chicken, and wanton soup. I went for the dumplings first.

Time flew as I ate my dinner while continuing to catch up on the show. When the mid-season finale ended, I was tired enough to go to sleep. After I threw the trash out and put the leftovers in the fridge, I went to bed. Minion came up shortly after, waiting, as usual, until I was half asleep to jump onto my pillow. She danced around, then settled into my hair and purred. Listening to that sound was the most relaxing part of my day.

Eleven

IT WAS MONDAY MORNING. I woke up feeling fabulous; I guess sleep *was* that restorative. It was the best I'd felt in a few weeks if I was being honest. I threw the covers off, placing my feet on the cold floor. It was a pleasurable cold, not the kind that numbs toes on impact. I padded to the bathroom and looked in the mirror before beginning my routine. Even my reflection looked better; the dark circles I noticed yesterday were fading. I smiled and went about my day.

Traffic sucked, as usual, but it didn't seem to bother me today. I danced as I drove, bopping my head to party music.

I walked into the office, and Barb was already at her desk. It dawned on me that she liked to be early enough to get situated before starting to work. I liked that.

"Morning!" I said to her with a smile.

"Good morning, Britney! How was your weekend?"

"Had its ups and downs. How was yours?" I asked as I walked over to her desk.

"I spent a lot of time thinking," she responded.

"Oh?" I raised an eyebrow and smirked.

Barb blushed. "I've decided I'm going to make sure Jim knows who he's flirting with. What have I got to lose?"

The shock was clear on my face. "I'm proud of you for putting yourself out there, Barb!"

"Me too. And scared. I hope he doesn't reject me."

"We're all afraid of rejection," I comforted, hearing Ben's voice in my head as I spoke the words. Was I already reverting to who I worked so diligently to be? "Seriously, Barb, I'm really proud of you. You're blossoming here."

"Thanks, Britney. I agree. I enjoy working for you," she beamed.

"Glad to hear it," I replied, patting her hand and smiling. I turned and walked into my office.

I performed my daily ritual of booting up, and Barb added something to it. While I waited for my computer, she came in and handed me my messages. I thanked her.

"Hey, Barb," I called, stopping her at the doorway.

"Yes?"

"I like this. Let's keep it going." I smiled at her.

"You got it," she said before turning and leaving.

I looked down at the messages in my hand, smiled, and got to work. I was reorganizing the pink pages that Barb handed over when Julie called my cell phone.

"Hey, girl!"

"Hey, Brit! Happy Monday! How was your weekend?"

"Eh, it was a weekend. How was yours?"

"Not so great. That's part of why I'm calling." Her voice remained cheerful. I internally panicked. "Nothing's wrong, I promise. I know that's where you just went." She giggled.

"Are you gonna tell me or make me wonder?" I half joked.

"Brian misses you."

"I miss him too. Why didn't he call or text to tell me himself?"

"He's grounded. I took his phone."

"He's *what?*" I was incredulous. That kid was a goody-goody and geek. There was no way he'd done something to get in that kind of trouble. "Jules, he's a geek. What could he possibly have done to deserve that?"

Julie audibly gulped. "He was doing homework and got frustrated."

"Isn't that normal?"

"Well, yeah, but…"

"Jules, what? Tell me." I started to worry about her more than Brian.

"He cursed out a teacher via email. I didn't know he'd even sent it, I swear! Then the teacher called me and I freaked. Brit, I'm so embarrassed and mad!" She spoke in a sort of choked rapid-fire. Her tone was a mix of anger and that breaking thing voices do when the person is about to cry.

"Wow…" I was dumbfounded. To know such a sweet kid would do something like this knocked me back a bit. Could he be hiding a dark side like me? "Jules, I'm so sorry! Want me to talk to him?"

She let out a relieved sigh. "You took the words right out of my mouth. I know it's a lot to ask, but I wouldn't be if I didn't think you could help. I'm just mom to him, so nothing I say helps."

"We were kids once too, Jules," I pointed out. "And for real? 'A lot to ask?' Girl, please! You're like family to me. Of course I'll talk to him. Well, I'll try. Just because he likes me doesn't mean he'll tell me what's going on."

"I know, and I appreciate it. Thanks, Brit."

"You need to stop thanking me for adoring you," I replied with a strained giggle.

We chatted a few minutes longer about work-related stuff and set up a day and time for dinner at her place before hanging up. I sighed as I tapped the button to end the call. I hoped Brian wasn't like me; this isn't a way to live. Is it?

When I was his age, I'd already known what I was and taught myself to hide it. I got better as I got older, but to look at me now is like watching a train wreck. I have emotions I never thought I'd have. I want to out myself to a cop—a fucking COP! And I was considering that if Brian needed my help learning how to be a killer, I'd help him. No. That can't happen. I'd already become more of a danger to those I love.

And poor Brian! How would he even process that, if it was true? Am I freaking out about nothing? Nope, this isn't real. It can't be.

I realized I was emphatically shaking my head at my internal conversation and felt a sudden embarrassment. We all talked to ourselves and had internal voices, right? I convinced myself that Barb would have said something if she'd seen me. Then I shifted gears, and put my focus on my company, and got to work.

There were messages from two or three clients and another half-dozen from applicants. The clients were always priority, so I called them first. I picked up the receiver and took a deep breath. Today was looking to be an annoyance, but I was determined not to allow that to happen. I dialed the number on the paper and became Britney Cage, CEO.

After I was finished pleasing clients, I called the applicants back. Two didn't answer but the rest scheduled appointments. I entered the information I had into the database so Barb could finish gathering what was needed for their arrivals. Control issues dictated that I kept some things for myself to do. Besides, I'd be bored all day if I only had to return calls and emails.

And, just like that, I was. There were no appointments scheduled until after lunch, and today wasn't a typical busy Monday. I was grateful for the respite but had no clue what to do with myself. I didn't want to take focus off of work until I got home later; it's was the only thing that seems to help me stay somewhat grounded. So I decided to run some database maintenance by cleaning up the inactive employees.

I'd had the software custom built because I have my own way of doing things and most programs aren't very user-friendly. I wanted it to be easy enough for beginners but detailed enough that I could keep track of everything I needed, including client information. It was also made so that I could simply run a query with minimal parameters. I clicked some checkboxes and then the "run" button. In a matter of seconds, the inactive employees were marked and wouldn't show as available. We ran this query for clients, too, usually on a monthly basis. For employees, it was a weekly thing.

I still had plenty of time before lunch—just under an hour. So I did what anyone else who's bored at work would do. I clacked on the keyboard for a few seconds, and the Netflix welcome screen popped up. It was easier than falling down a YouTube hole and a lot less time consuming. I couldn't be late coming back because I had an appointment scheduled for 1:30 p.m. and needed the time between it and lunch to prepare.

A cartoon later and it was lunchtime. I went home today because I hadn't thought to bring anything with me and was craving the remaining Bourbon chicken in my fridge. I was glad I took an hour because I hated to eat and run; an hour afforded me the ability to enjoy my food. And that I did. Craving satisfied, I went back to the office and got on with the rest of my work hours.

The next thing I knew, it was 5 p.m. My workday now over, I was in the same good mood I was in this morning. By the time I got home, I believed that I was getting back to my usual self.

Then Shae called. A wicked grin spread across my face before I answered.

"Shae! How are you?"

"I'm great. How are you?"

"Same. What's going on?"

"I've been working on the way I talk at work like you taught me, and the boss actually complimented me for it! Can you believe it? I didn't think I could do it. But, wow, you were so right about the exhausting part. Does it get easier?"

I needed the things I taught her to work; my plans for her were finally taking shape. "Congratulations! I can believe it because it's worked for me. And no, it doesn't get easier—it gets more manageable."

"I don't know if that makes me feel better, but thanks. Can I take you to lunch to show my appreciation?"

"No," I said, "but we can go to lunch because we're friends."

Shae snickered. "Perfect! When is good?"

"Hmm, I'm actually not sure. Can I text you tomorrow?"

"Sounds good. Thanks again, Brit. Not just for your help, but for being a friend to someone like me."

"I get how hard friends are to make. No thanks needed."

"Bye," Shae said and hung up.

What did she mean by "someone like her"?

I was lying about not knowing when would be a good day, but she didn't need to know that. I needed to figure out how to get her to tell me more about her life. I wasn't the only one who felt something off about her now, so I had to find out. She'd trusted me enough to come clean about her identity change. I would get her to open up about the rest, one way or another.

I set my phone down in the kitchen and went to change into something more comfortable. When I came back, I pulled the rest of last night's Chinese out and heated it up. After feeding Minion, I looked at my phone to see a missed call from Stu. He didn't send a text though. Weird. I debated calling him back for whatever time was left on the microwave. The beeping interrupted that debate and curiosity got the better of me. I let my food stay there and called Stu back.

"Hi," he answered somberly.

"Hey. I saw you called…" This was awkward and I hated it.

"Yeah. Brit, look, I don't know what's going on between us, but it sucks. How do we move past this?"

I opened my mouth to speak, but no sound came out. I tried again. "I-I don't really know."

"Me either. Do you think we even *can* move past this?"

"Yes. What about…No, that's no good." I shook my head.

"What? I'll try anything. I miss you and I miss us. We have a great friendship and could have an even better relationship. Tell me."

"I was thinking therapy," I said, starting to giggle at how absurd friendship therapy sounded.

Stu snickered. "That sounds insane."

"And that's why I said it wouldn't be good. What about if we just talked about how we feel? Like, maybe establish clearer boundaries. Do you think that could work?" I missed him too and wanted this to not be the way it currently was.

"I'm willing to give it a try if you are," he replied, hopeful.

"Wouldn't have said it if I didn't mean it," I said and smiled.

"Good. Let's do that then." Stu went silent for a long while. "Stu, you still there?"

"Yeah, sorry, I didn't really know what else to say there."

I let out a nervous laugh. "I don't know either. I guess we hang up now?"

"I guess. I mean, if we don't have anything to say to each other."

"We're both way too nervous. I think we should talk again soon." I spoke as evenly as I could but still sounded strained.

"Sounds good. Talk soon." Stu's voice sounded the same way mine did before he ended the call.

I took my food from the microwave and slumped into one of the chairs at the table to eat. Minion sat at my feet, loudly asking me to share, but I somehow managed not to spoil her even more. The Princess wasn't happy about that, though she did allow me to finish my food to her song.

Back to feeling shitty, I sat on the couch intending to finish catching up on that show. But as soon as I turned the TV on, I realized I wouldn't be able to concentrate. So I went upstairs and opened my safe. This time, I sat on the floor and enjoyed the view. I let my thoughts wander to potential ways to kill Shae.

I may not have had a precise reason yet—or a disposal method—but I knew she'd die by my hands. The vial of ketamine sat on a shelf about eye-level from my seat on the floor, next to the box of syringes I'd picked up from a local drug store. The light reflected off the bottle, making it appear to wink at me. A grin started to take up the corners of my mouth. My eyes shifted to the boxes of contractor bags and gloves on the next shelf down, and the grin grew.

From there, my thoughts wandered to taping Shae's wrists and ankles, then taping her to a table. The table would have to be one that wouldn't soak up her blood. Or maybe I could cut contractor bags open and cover the table with them. That meant I'd have to cover the floor too. This was becoming a workable plan. I just needed to figure out the details of how, why, and where, and disposal. The KKD of Shae was finally revealing itself.

The grin took up my whole face.

Twelve

WEDNESDAY ARRIVED, AND I found myself excited to see Danielle for lunch. Before that, though, I had to work. And I had to call Shae about lunch. I'd forgotten yesterday; I was too distracted with visions of stabbing and dismembering her.

I'd dismembered the McLaughlin sisters, but that was the only way to grind their bodies into sausage. I wondered how human sausage tasted. Did the people who bought it suspect something was wrong? That it wasn't pork sausage? Then I wondered what human meat tasted like. I was a fan of Hannibal Lecter, but it was just a rumor that he was based on a real doctor in Mexico. I didn't know anyone I could ask. Maybe I'd find out for myself with one of my kills. Hell, maybe it would even be Shae.

About an hour after I'd gotten into the office, Danielle texted me with the name of the restaurant she wanted to meet at. It was a lot closer to my office than hers, but she didn't seem to care. We agreed to meet at 1 p.m., that way there would be less traffic for her to combat on her drive back.

Then I texted Shae.

Tomorrow and Friday are open.

I have a meeting tomorrow. Friday is better.

You got it. Anywhere special?
Nah. Pizza, tacos…I don't care.
Cool. We can decide Friday then.
Great!

She didn't ask why I was late getting back to her, and I wasn't sure I cared if it did bother her. I only needed her to trust me for a little while longer. I didn't want this to drag out for months like the sisters had. No, Shae would die in weeks. Of that, I was certain.

I muddled through the morning by meeting with applicants. My last interview ended by 12:20 p.m., allowing me to leave the office a few minutes earlier than planned. I grabbed my purse and locked up after myself. Barb had taken her lunch around noon, after announcing the applicant, and would be back while I was still out.

Leaving the parking lot, I was glad we'd chosen the later time. Not only was there less traffic, but the day seemed to be moving faster. I thought about taking a later lunch every Tuesday through Thursday. I decided to wait and see how the rest of the week played out before committing to anything.

I found the place easily enough—it was a food truck with an attached roof and blue picnic tables. I parked in the lot and got out. The weather was almost as gross as yesterday. Typical Tampa in late spring. It felt like summer most of the year anyway, so this wasn't really much different than a November day. As I walked over to look at the menu on the side of the truck, Danielle puled in and parked. She hopped out of her car and rushed me like we hadn't seen each other in forever. She knocked us both off balance when she hugged me.

"It's so great to see you!" Her face lit up as she grinned.

"It's great to see you too! It's been a while since we last hung out just me and you. What's going on?"

"We can catch up while we eat. I'm starving." She walked closer to the truck, eying the menu.

In less than three minutes, we'd both ordered and looked around for a place to sit with our drinks. We had our choice of the four tables since we were the only ones there. This place wasn't in the best of neighborhoods to leave a vehicle in, so we chose the one closest to where we'd parked.

"I like this roof," Danielle said as we sat. It was white, like the base color of the truck, with lights and fans.

"Me too. It's a fun color scheme they have here." I looked around as I spoke, then took a sip of my iced tea. "Shae called me to tell me that the boss complimented her on her ability to be tactful."

Danielle grinned. "Yep! Do you know what that means? It means I get to back off and do my damn job." Her eyes sparkled.

"That's awesome! How far behind are you?"

"I never really was. I'd stay late and my family hated it. So, the next time we get together for lunch or dinner, it's my treat. A thank you from the family." She was so happy, I couldn't bring myself to argue.

I laughed. "You're all welcome, but it's...well, I'm not gonna argue. What else is going on?"

Before Danielle could answer, our names were called at the window. We grabbed our food and sat back down. Danielle bit into her tacos before she did anything else.

"Oh wow," she moaned, "that's a good taco!"

I bit into mine and drooled. It was probably the best chorizo taco I'd ever had. We'd eaten two tacos each before resuming our conversation.

"Brad got a new position at work. Same worksite but different title and office; he's in IT now. Came with a nice raise too. Sophie is doing well in school, but I can't believe kids bully each other so early. She comes home sad that they're mean to her, so we have her working extra time with her teachers so she doesn't fall behind. We may have to get her a tutor, but it hasn't come to that yet." Danielle finished another taco. "What's new with you?"

"Not much, really. Julie's kid, Brian, is having trouble with school too. She asked me to come over for dinner to talk to him." I shrugged and finished my food. "Can I ask you something about Shae?"

Danielle finished chewing and swallowed. "I think I know what you're gonna ask. You feel something off about her, right?"

"You do too?" I found this development intriguing.

"Yep. She's totally hiding something. Has she hinted at anything to you?"

"No." I shook my head. "It's weird. Like, she's totally honest with me about some things though. Like where she moved from and why."

I wasn't going to tell Danielle everything; it wasn't my place. And I needed to maintain everyone's ignorance about what I was. Once Shae goes missing, people will already look at her small crew of friends like we know something. I already knew what my story would be.

"I know where she's from, and she mentioned a stalker," Danielle said, "But I never prodded her about it. It's not my business and I figure she'll tell me if she wants to."

I looked at my watch. It was 1:46 p.m.—time for both of us to get back to work.

"Yeah, I have to go too," Danielle acknowledged.

We stood, threw our trash away, and hugged again.

"We should do this more often," I said.

"We should."

"Tell Brad and Sophie I say hi."

"You know it. Love you, girl."

"Love you too," I replied. "Text you later."

We separated, went to our vehicles, and left. Traffic was picking up but still better than the usual lunch rush. I thought again about taking lunch later in the day, but the thoughts disappeared when a fun party song came on. I sang and danced my way back to the office. I even walked in bopping my head around.

Barb giggled at me. "Welcome back. I take it your lunch date was fun."

"You know it! How was your lunch?"

"It was…interesting." She smirked and blushed simultaneously. "I called Jim and he asked me out. He said he knew it was me the whole time."

"That's so great! Congratulations! When are you going out?" I was truly happy for her. Someone had to be positive of what they wanted, and it couldn't be me right now.

"Tomorrow for lunch. I'm excited and nervous. What do I wear? How do I act?"

"You dress like you normally would. It's the middle of a weekday, and he knows what you do for a living." I smiled, thinking more about how to encourage her. "Act like yourself. He's already talked to you how many times now? Barb, you'll do just fine."

I hugged her on my way into my office. She gratefully hugged me back.

"You're a lot cooler than I expected, Britney. Thanks for being you."

"Thanks? And you're welcome?" I wasn't sure what she meant by that, but I was grateful she didn't know the me I kept hidden.

Back at my desk, the rest of the day flew by. This later lunch thing could be good. Regardless, I couldn't jump the shark just yet. I needed more experience with it. As much of a creature of habit as I am, it would change some of those habits, so being sure it would actually be better was a necessity.

With the little amount of work I had left now completed, I got myself set up to have another productive day tomorrow. I laid out my planner and other paperwork, all in some kind of order that I'd easily be able to explain to Barb or Julie should the need arise. I admired my workload organization and wished my brain would clear up enough so I could be like this with my killer and personal lives too.

I grabbed my purse and headed out the door, saying "Goodnight" to Barb as I left. It wasn't even five yet, but end of day traffic had already started. While I was at a red light, I called Joe to see what he was up to.

"Britney! It's good to hear your voice, kid! How are you?"

"I'm okay. Hey, Joe, what are your dinner plans?"

"It's already been made, but there's more than enough. Why don't you come on over?"

"Sounds great! Be there soon."

"Drive safe," Joe said and hung up.

Thirteen

AS I PULLED UP to Joe's house about fifteen minutes later, the front door opened. Joe was in the doorway waving and smiling. It had been a while since I last saw him. We were long overdue, usually meeting up once a week for lunch or just a chat.

I parked my Jeep and hopped out. Concern showed on Joe's face as I walked closer.

"What's wrong?" I asked.

"It's been weeks since we last talked, Britney. I'm just concerned, is all."

I wrapped him in a hug, and he hugged back. When we let go Joe stepped back to let me in and closed the door. He drifted behind me as I walked.

Dinner smelled amazing; Joe chuckled at me sniffing the air like a dog.

"Is that pot roast?" The excitement in my voice combined with the sniffing made it obvious I loved pot roast.

"It is. Marsha made it while I was at work."

I spun around to face him, meaning to mother him, but he looked the happiest he had in some time. I smiled instead.

"Who's Marsha?" I prodded, keeping the tone light and playful.

"New housekeeper," Joe replied as we walked into the dining room.

Joe sat down in his chair at the end of the table. I pulled a chair out on the side, sitting at an angle to Joe's left. There was a place setting waiting for me. I took a sip of water before beginning my inquiry into Marsha.

"Joan quit for personal reasons. Her daughter got injured at work, and she went to take care of her. She didn't know when she'd be back"—Joe paused to drink some water—"so she gave her notice. That was it. I tried to ask questions to see what I could do to help, but Joan wouldn't have it. Said something about I'd been too good to her over the years, and it was unnecessary."

I shook my head. "Wow. I hope everything's alright. When did this happen?"

"A month ago. No big deal." Joe picked up his fork and dug into his pot roast.

I, too, picked a fork up, going for my mashed potatoes first. They were so creamy and delicious, I almost forgot we were having a conversation.

"So, tell me about Marsha. Where'd you find her? How long has she been doing this kind of thing? What's she—"

"I've been doing this kind of thing my whole life," she said, walking into the room smiling. Marsha was a cute kid. I didn't mean she was a child, but she didn't look like she was even the same age as me.

"And how long is that?" I was snarky. There was no way she'd be able to handle Joe by herself. One month wasn't long enough to tell.

"25 years, give or take." She shrugged.

I almost choked on my mashed potatoes. I wanted to know her life story, but now wasn't the time to be bitchy about it. I was here for Joe, not her.

"Oh wow. So, how did you find Joe here?" I motioned with the handle of my fork as I continued to eat.

"Through the agency I worked for. Your buddy Joe chose me from those he'd interviewed and then brought me on direct." Marsha smiled at me. She had shoulder-length dark hair and green eyes. She seemed nice, but I was meeting her for the first time. I didn't get any weird feelings, but I also knew Joe well enough to know that he'd had her thoroughly checked out. I smiled back at her and dug back into my food, intent on finishing my plate.

"Well, Marsha, you make a mean pot roast. Maybe I'll ask for tips." I winked. She giggled and went back to doing something in the kitchen.

Joe flashed me a disapproving look.

"What? I'm only trying to look out for you." I tried not to choke on the bits of food still in my mouth.

"I know. And you know I'm more than capable of looking out for myself," he admonished before going back to his dinner.

"I'm sorry. So, what else has been going on? You said you went to work…how's that going?"

Joe ignored me until we'd both cleared our plates. He set his fork down and steepled his fingers.

"It's going well." He looked happy and content, though I couldn't tell if that was from dinner, work, or a combination of both.

"That's good. I take it you took it slow and easy." I sounded like a mother making sure her child did as they were supposed to.

"I did. I'm much older than you and have been running my practice long enough—"

"To still ignore doctor's orders," I finished. We both laughed.

"Fair enough," Joe remarked, still smirking. "What's been going on with you?"

"Where do you want me to start?" I huffed and chugged the remaining water in my glass and let fly. By the time I was done telling him almost everything, Joe looked sad.

I noticed the frown. "What's wrong?"

"You. Why won't you let yourself be happy? And don't lie to me like you've no doubt lied to everyone else."

Shit. I was stuck. I couldn't well tell him I was a killer. I had to come up with some other line of bullshit and fast.

"I just can't. Yes, I love him and he loves me. And that's why I think I'll fuck it up. Good things don't really last long with me." I pouted.

Joe reached over and put a comforting hand on my shoulder. "I'm a good thing in your life, and I've been here how long now?"

He fell for it; I was safe. He also wasn't wrong. Joe was a good thing in my life that somehow I hadn't fucked up.

I put my hand on his and looked him in the eyes. "Thanks, Joe. For everything."

"Bah!" He waved me off with his other hand as he took back the one he had on my shoulder.

Marsha came back out, pie plate in hand. "Cherry pie?" She set it down on the table, and I noticed it was still steaming.

"Wow, okay. Thanks, Marsha," I said, impressed.

"Of course," she replied, taking up our dirty dishes. "I'll be right back with clean for you."

I looked at Joe, happily surprised. "She bakes pies too? Alright then."

Marsha came back, set the plates and forks, then served us each a fat slice of pie. My mouth watered again at the smell of the fresh pie.

"You sure know the way to someone's heart," I joked.

"I'm the oldest of six, so I learned how to cook early on." She looked at me, and all I could see in her eyes was happiness. I really did want to get to know her, but I recognized that I couldn't kill her and not draw attention. She's Joe's housekeeper; that would be more than bad form. Killing Alex was different because I'd found him first.

Marsha left Joe and me to enjoy our dessert. And enjoy we did. So much that we didn't even speak until we'd finished our slices.

"Damn! That girl can cook. Maybe I'll move in," I quipped.

"There's more than enough room…" Joe's tone was serious.

"Joe…I-I couldn't…"

"I know. It just gets lonely sometimes."

"But you have Marsha here."

"She goes home every night around eight." Then he waved off whatever he was about to say.

I didn't know how to respond, so I took hold of his hand that was on the table and held it for a long time. Joe smiled at me in return, squeezing my hand.

My phone chimed, taking my attention from Joe. I pulled it from my purse to see a text from Stu.

Hey! Busy?

I'm at Joe's. Can I call you when I leave?

Yep

My face didn't use its inside voice again, and Joe noticed.

"Why so glum? Everything okay?"

"Yeah. Everything's fine," I said, pulling my face back together.

"You don't have to fake happy for me, Brit. You know that." He smiled and nodded, acknowledging the pain we were both feeling.

"Joe, I'm sorry for being such a terrible friend. Can we do this more?"

"Of course we can!" he said as he stood. "But right now, I need to use the restroom."

I picked up our dirty dishes and took them into the kitchen. Marsha was wiping the island down and picked her head up when she heard me.

"Oh, you don't have to do that!" She dropped the towel onto the counter and came over.

I walked past her attempted grab, smirking. "I need to not think, so yes, I do. How about I just set them in the sink?"

"Deal," she replied. "Anything you wanna talk about?"

"Nah. Thanks though." I set the stack in the sink as agreed and walked back into the dining room. Joe was waiting for me, my purse in his hands.

"I know you better than you sometimes realize, Britney," he said as he handed my purse over.

"You do. If I'm being honest, it kinda scares me," I said, forming a half-smile.

"Nothing scares you except your feelings." He was being nice about it; feelings terrified me. But I wasn't about to say it out loud.

"Fair enough. Walk me to the door, would you, old man?" I smirked.

He patted his belly. "I am getting old, aren't I? I'll be 60 soon…pushing Medicare age," he laughed.

I stopped short of opening the door and hugged Joe good-bye.

"I love you, Britney," he said, "and yes, let's do this more often. As long as you promise to be nice to Marsha."

I snickered with amusement. "Yes, sir."

I let go and walked out.

Fourteen

INSIDE MY JEEP, I pulled my phone from my purse and called Stu back.

"Hey! What's up?"

"That was fast. I didn't interrupt anything, did I?"

I shifted and pulled out of Osten's driveway. "Nope. I was just finishing dinner at Joe's. He's got a new housekeeper, and I gotta tell you, that girl can *cook*!"

Stu chuckled. "Well, I'm glad I wasn't calling about dinner tonight, then. How about tomorrow?"

"Uh, I…maybe? What happened to us taking a step back?"

"I know, but—"

"Stu, no." I physically bit my tongue. "We need to respect the boundaries. Maybe next week we can do dinner. I have to think about it."

Stu sighed heavily. "Okay, Brit. You got it. I respect you and will respect your boundaries, whether I understand them or not."

"Thank you," I replied, heavyhearted.

"Well, have a good night," Stu said, sounding dejected. I hoped we'd both stop feeling so shitty, but for now, it was all we could really do.

I needed to relax, but I also needed to conduct research. So, I used the Bluetooth to call someone else.

"Hey, Brit!" Shae said between bites of something.

"Shit, I'm sorry. Did I catch you at a bad time?" I faked concern.

"Not at all! What's up?"

"Wanna meet up for drinks?"

"I'm in pajamas. But I've got all kinds of wine and liquor. Wanna come here? " Shae asked.

"Sure! On my way." A wicked smile spread across my face as I ended the call. Maybe if I got her buzzed, she'd open up more about her life and why we all felt something off about her.

I checked my mirrors, then changed lanes so I could make a right and circle back away from my neighborhood toward Shae's. She only lived ten miles from my house, but I had already been headed south. I was between Joe's house and mine when I called her.

Twenty minutes later, I pulled into the driveway of her rental. I guessed her car was in the garage since I talked to her and she said she was here. I shut the engine off and hopped down, locking my Jeep as I walked to the front door.

It swung open and Shae bear-hugged me. "It's so good to see you! Thanks for coming over!" She was definitely tipsy; she never greeted me like this.

Shae walked away from the open door, and I walked in, locking it behind me. She lived in a sketchy spot, caught between a bunch of burglaries and stolen cars.

"Where's your car?" I asked. Not that I was concerned, but she needed to believe I was.

"Garage," she replied from the kitchen. "I'm making martinis. Want one?"

"Extra dirty!" I said as I walked the lower floor of her place, starting with where I'd come in. It was cute. Smaller than mine, a weird shade of tan covering the walls. The floor was mostly beige carpet with the exception of the tiny kitchen and half bath.

I was looking up the stairs when Shae came out and handed me a martini in a red plastic cup. I looked at it and sniffed. "Mmm, smells good."

"Extra dirty," she slurred.

"How long have you been drinking?" I took a sip and was pleasantly surprised.

"I dunno. Like three hours maybe?" Shae didn't stumble and her slur was minimal.

"Wow. After three hours, I'm usually pretty lit. You can handle your alcohol." I took a healthy gulp from my cup.

"Well, when you've lived a life like mine, drinking becomes the only thing that gives a sense of normalcy."

I finished my drink and walked toward the kitchen. "Why don't you tell me about it after I make a pitcher or something?"

"Ooo! Good idea! Want help?"

"Only to show me where everything is." I grinned.

Shae led the way to the kitchen, bumping into me a couple times because it was the size of a full bathroom. We giggled every time.

"Small, right? I'm so glad it's just me. I don't mind the size except when I have people over," Shae commented.

"Is that often?"

"You're the first person to be here, so I guess no." Shae started to sway a little. She leaned up against the fridge while I slid past her to make the pitcher of Martinis.

"Aw, you like me!" I mimicked an actress in a role; I couldn't remember who said it or even the movie I'd seen it in. I put my hand on my chest. "You *really* like me!"

Shae cackled gleefully and clapped. "You're good at that. Do it again!"

I laughed. "If I could, I would. That bit only comes out at mostly the right times."

I poured the vodka and olive juice into the pitcher and stirred. A container this large wasn't ideal to shake. I threw in a handful of ice for good measure and stirred a little more. Shae's eyes lit up.

"You got a bowl or something for me to put the olives in?"

"I have forks. We can just eat them from the jar."

"That works," I said as I picked up the pitcher and followed Shae into the living room. Shae put the olive jar on the coffee table, and I filled our cups to the halfway point. Shae tipped hers in my direction as I sat down. I picked mine up and we "clinked," the plastic giving a squeak, and we drank.

Shae set her cup down on a coaster, then grabbed the jar and a fork. "You know, if we don't finish the martinis, I can just pour it back into here and then the olives will soak."

"Shit. I'd never thought of that. Great idea! We should soak olives in martinis for a party!" I saluted her with my cup and drank again. In truth, I really never had thought of that.

Shae munched on the olives, looking lost in space.

"What's going on? Talk to me," I prodded.

"I just…I dunno. I just feel like I'm being fake , but I know I'm not. At work, I mean. And then mshfsh called…" The mumble caught my attention.

"You're not being fake. You're learning tact, there's a difference," I pointed out. "I don't think that's the problem, though. Who called?"

"Michael." Shae hung her head, an expression of embarrassment on her face.

I drank. Shae followed suit.

"Who's Michael?"

"The gang guy. I mean…my ex."

Now we were getting somewhere. "What did he say? Did he threaten you? I'll call Stu…" I was getting better at the acting bit; more like I was getting back to being good. I even started to pull my phone out. She put her hand on mine, pushing it back into my purse.

"No, I'm okay. He did threaten me, but he doesn't know where I am or what name I'm using. I'm safe, I promise."

"That's not okay, Shae! Really, let me call Stu, and you can at least have it on record that—"

"Brit, no. But thanks for caring."

She didn't know that I saw this as an opportunity—for myself, of course. Though, it would be a little more difficult if she didn't report it at all. She'd come around; I'd make sure of it.

I changed tack. "How did he even get your number?"

Shae hung her head. "I left it for him when I left."

"Hang on, let me piece this together. You met him here in Tampa. Then you followed him to Chicago. There you found out he's in a gang, got stalked by another gang member, never called the cops or feds, and just took off. But not before getting a new phone number and giving it to him. Then, when you got back here, you changed your name?"

It sounded so stupid and backwards as I said it out loud.

Shae made a noise but no words came out. Her head dropped and trembled a little.

"Shae?" I set my cup on the table and rested a hand on her knee. Her shoulders started bobbing. I slid closer and held her. She cried for a few minutes and wiped her nose with the back of her hand before trying to talk.

"The c-cops"—she took a deep breath—"are on the gang's payroll. I couldn't call them and stay alive. And I didn't want to call the feds because I was fucking terrified! Maybe I've watched too many movies or something, but I didn't want to be just whisked away and never talk to those I knew again. So I called around and found someone who didn't have contacts to the gang to change my name and stuff. Shaelyn White has only had a paper trail for two years."

I held her closer and thought more about this new detail. What would happen when she's gone? Could I pin it on her ex? It sounded like it would be easy enough. I needed to know more but couldn't be pushy. So I leaned over and picked our cups off the table, handing hers over. Shae took a long drink, emptying her cup. I took it and refilled it, then handed it back. She nodded her thanks.

When She took the cup from her mouth, I could more clearly see how puffy and red her eyes were. Her face was flushed, and her bottom lip still quivered. She wiped her nose with the back of her hand again.

"Thanks, Brit. You're a good friend."

"As your friend, I ask you to consider filing a report. You don't know how desperate he is, Shae. He could come here looking for you. And thanks, I try to be a good friend." I do try, or I did. I had let Joe fall by the wayside and needed to get back on track. But Shae? I didn't care about her. She was nothing more to me than my next kill. And maybe a bit of a student. But I couldn't let that get in the way.

Shae hugged me. Inside I cringed, but I hugged her back. Then she changed the subject, an obvious attempt to get her mind off reality.

"Did I ever tell you I have a fascination with cannibalism?"

Fifteen

"YOU HAVE A WHAT?" I wasn't shocked but I also was.

Shae nodded. "Yeah, I've always thought about how expensive death is and wondered if I could be a food source instead of cremated or buried. Plus, it's interesting to know that humans eat other humans."

Why did Dahmer have to die? Aren't there cannibal tribes somewhere in the world? What did human meat even taste like? My brain swirled. Shae had just given me the perfect disposal method. I had a lot of research ahead of me.

I regained my composure. "Shae? What was your name before you changed it?"

"Do we have to talk about this now?" Shae whimpered, not wanting to get back to the meat and potatoes of what she obviously needed to finish talking about. It was just as much for her good as it was for mine.

"Yes. You'll feel better."

"But who I was before doesn't matter." She paused to think. "Or maybe it does. The only person who knows the whole story is Michael, and it *is* killing me to keep it all in."

That wasn't the only killing she'd experience with me.

"Sally Walker was my real name. I kept my birth date and changed everything else. Dyed my hair red, my eyes aren't this color…" She pulled an eyelid up and removed a green contact lens, showed it to me, then put it back in.

"Okay, that's gross. You could do some serious damage to your eye doing that. Yes, I wear contacts too. It's one of my biggest fears to get an eye infection because I didn't clean my lenses well enough." I shivered.

Shae finished her drink and swallowed. "Sorry. I know but I guess I don't care much right now. I feel like shit about my life as a whole. I fucked up big, and now it's coming back for me." Her voice broke. She didn't cry this time; she got mad. Yay for drunken mood swings.

"You made a mistake, Shae; no big deal. Unless you killed someone, I'm sure karma has already fucked you over," I returned with a grin.

She shrugged. "Good point."

"Look, you'll get through this. You have me and the others. Except Heather. I should call her or something. Anyway, you get what I'm saying. You have us to help you."

"Eh, maybe. I don't plan to tell the others. You're the only one I fully trust."

"I'll take that. And I'll keep your secret," I said, making an X over my heart. I'd keep hers like I kept mine. She wouldn't be alive long enough for anyone to figure hers out anyhow.

Having pulled off what I set out to do, I checked my watch. Shae saw and put her cup down.

"Thanks for hanging out with me," she said.

"Thanks for inviting me over. Girl's night soon?"

Shae's face flushed again. "I don't know. Let me see how I feel. Maybe just you and me could do lunch or dinner instead?"

"Just let me know. Still on for lunch Friday?"

"You know it!"

I stood, picked my purse up, and walked to the door. Shae came with me. I hugged her and walked out, stopping on the walkway to listen as she locked the door. I got into my Jeep and headed home.

I pushed the thoughts of Stu away in favor of formulating something resembling a plan for killing Shae. She'd given me everything but a reason so far. That was fine; I'd figure one out. Now that I knew she wanted to be eaten, I decided that a dedicated killing knife was a necessity. As for the rest of her body, well, I'd feed it to the gators. This way, more than one species could have a full stomach by obeying her wishes. But I still needed to come up with the where on my own.

Once I got into my house, I battled Minion's attempts to trip me and fed her. Then I went upstairs and opened my safe. I moved things around, gathering the supplies in an easy to grab spot. I still needed the knife and a holder or case for it. I'd put everything in the bag once I had the knife. I didn't have a reason for that choice; it just was.

I changed and climbed into bed, my thoughts drifting to what I wanted my knife to look like.

The next thing I knew, it was morning. I could tell because my alarm screamed at me. I shut it off and rolled out of bed, feeling less than stellar. I was just tired and I'd get over it. I brushed my teeth and went down to make coffee before doing anything else. Caffeine would be my savior today.

I opened an incognito browser window on my phone and searched for different knives and coatings on the walk to the kitchen. I set it down on the counter next to the coffee maker and did what I had to do to have the black goodness start brewing. After pressing the button, I picked my phone back up and sat at the table, continuing to search while the coffee brewed.

I flipped through about three dozen photos before finding the color scheme I liked. When I did, I went to the website for the coating, and found a dealer. There was a call option, but it was 7 a.m. So I took a screenshot and searched though Buck knives.

I found one I liked and that would fit in the bag nicely. I didn't like the handle though and noticed that they make custom knives. The online store was also certified to Cerakote. The custom one didn't come with a case, but those were easy enough to buy on the same site. I was also sure a local dealer would have one suitable. Then the coffee maker stopped its popping noises. I stood and poured my mug and went back up to shower, pausing long enough to sip. I didn't even care that I burned my mouth.

I emptied my first mug long before I reached the top of the stairs. I figured I'd refill once I was out of the shower but would decide then. It was too late to jog and I was too tired anyway, so I took a shower and grabbed more coffee after. It felt like there wasn't going to be enough caffeine for the day. I resolved to go to bed early and see if that helped. I was convinced the exhaustion was from being up late the past few days. I refused to think emotions were what was truly kicking my ass.

I walked through the door to Passing Through, greeted Barb, and shifted gears. I had work to do—in the office and for pleasure. And today's first task was to place an order for my kill knife. Once my computer was fully booted, that was exactly what I did. It took about forty minutes to select the blade, handle, and coating colors I wanted. I clicked the submit button on the order page after entering my card info, and that was it.

I had grown more excited to kill Shae and more awake. I was glad for the endorphin rush.

I turned to the part of the desk where I'd laid out my work for today and got to it. I was in the middle of typing an email when the phone on my desk rang.

"This is Britney Cage."

"Hey, Brit!"

"Hi, Ben. You haven't invoiced me yet," I growled.

"I know, but I have an idea. I need a receptionist part time and I thought you could help me out with that, and I'd let the last visit go. Kind of like a barter system, if you will. You have something I need and I gave what you needed."

"Your offer sounds fair," I replied. "Tell me what you need."

As Ben listed his requirements, pay rate, and hours, I took notes.

"You got it. Thanks, Ben. Talk soon."

I was glad I didn't have to actually pay him, considering I felt that I didn't get what I needed from him. He'd done nothing more than tell me what I already knew, mostly.

I shrugged the memory of that last session off and got back to work. I wanted the day to end already; I had dinner plans.

To say I was looking forward to dinner with Julie and her family was an understatement. But I was also anxious about it. We'd planned this more so I could talk to Brian about his outburst at the teacher than for us to have a chance to catch up.

I still thought Brian might have a dark side. But I hoped he didn't. Not just for my own selfish reasons but for him too. He had been a good kid up until now. Maybe it was just a flare-up of frustration that caused him to send that email to his teacher. There was only one way to know for sure.

After lunch, I texted Julie to check that our plans were still moving forward. She replied that they were. I didn't bother asking if I could bring anything. She'd say no, and I'd still bring dessert or wine or both. I even wanted to stop at a bookstore and grab books for Brian, but it would look like I was rewarding him for getting suspended. And that would piss Julie off.

Four forty-five p.m. and it was time to start packing up. As I did, I called for Barb.

"Yes?" she asked, standing in the doorway.

"How did your date go? I totally forgot to ask. And you didn't offer details."

Barb blushed. "It was a good time. Jim's really nice. We're going to dinner tomorrow night."

"That's great to hear! Do you want to leave early to go home and change or anything?"

"No, thanks. We have reservations at 7:30, so I'll have enough time to go home first."

"Okay. Well, if you change your mind, just let me know," I said. I wondered why she didn't offer any details but chalked it up to her being shy.

"Thanks, Britney. I appreciate it. Have a good night," she said and walked back to her desk as I walked toward the door.

"You too."

There was a red Kia Optima with tinted windows parked next to me. It was running and I couldn't see inside of it. There were plenty of offices still open right now, but having recently been chased by a guy I interviewed, I was leery of this situation. I mentally noted the tag and eyed the window as I walked closer. I still couldn't see through to the inside, even this close. I huffed as I got into my Jeep, trying in vain to see into the car.

I shifted gears and left, more concerned about Brian than the possibility of being followed again. I watched my mirrors more than usual because I didn't want to bring any unwanted attention to Julie, Cody, or Brian. To come after me was one thing, but to go after my friends and family was asking for more than just being killed.

Halfway to Julie's house, my phone dinged. There was a text from an unknown number.

You didn't wave.

Sixteen

I STARED AT THE text long enough that cars behind me started honking. The light had turned green and I hadn't noticed.

Who is this?

I set the phone down in a cup holder and pulled up, having
missed the light. My knuckles were white, and my hands
started to hurt. Was I actually scared?

The light changed again, and I went. The text went unan-
swered even after I'd stopped at Publix and gotten to Julie's
house. I shrugged it off and grabbed the bags.

Brian opened the door and ran over to me, taking the bags
as I hopped down.

"Hey, Brit! I'm so happy to see you! Mom's been a real drag
lately. She grounded me," he said and dropped his shoulders.

"I heard. We can talk about that later, though. How are
you?" I hugged him, and he rested his cheek on my shoulder.

He didn't respond immediately; just kept his cheek against
me. I hugged tighter.

"Honestly? I don't know how I am. I'm frustrated and angry
and sad and scared. I just want these feelings to go away."

I pulled back and took his face in my hands. "You're a good
person, Brian. You just let your feelings get the better of you.

Let's go eat some good food, then you and me can chat after. What do you say?"

"I'd like that." He smiled and led the way inside.

In the kitchen, Julie looked up when we walked in. She stopped cutting vegetables and gave me a hug.

She eyed Brian setting the bags on the counter. "Brit, really?"

I giggled. "What? You should be used to this by now."

"I should," she responded, sounding cross with me. "What's in there?"

I walked over and took a bottle of wine from one of the bags, looking at Brian and nodding to the living room. He smiled his acknowledgment and left.

"Red Moscato is what we're having right now." I pulled two glasses from their cabinet and Julie got back to cutting. "What's for dinner?"

"Creamy lemon baked chicken and fresh steamed veggies."

I poured as she spoke and took a glass to her. Julie set the knife on the counter and we toasted.

"Thanks for agreeing to talk to Brian," she said after taking a sip.

"I love that kid; of course I'll talk to him. Has he said anything to you about why he did it?"

"No, but he isn't really talking to me, either. I just can't believe he—"

I held up my glass, signaling her to take another sip. "Look, I don't have kids and I don't want any, but I'm your friend and his. If he asks me to keep a secret, I will. And I understand why you're embarrassed and mad. I'm sure his reason is a normal-for-kids-in-middle-school one."

"Cheers to that!" Julie raised her glass and smiled again. We clinked, and Julie continued chopping. She had carrots, broccoli, and fresh green beans. I was getting hungrier by the minute.

"Can I help?"

"Yeah, by talking to Brian."

"Already told him we'd talk after dinner. Anything else I can do?" She waved the knife casually at the door.

"Nope. Dinner should be ready soon," she said without looking up.

So, I put the dessert of Boston cream pie in the fridge and placed the other bottle of wine on the dining room table. Then I went into the living room and found Cody just sitting down on the couch. When he saw me, he stopped and hugged me.

"Hey, Brit! How goes it?"

"Good, you?" I kissed his cheek.

"Great! Work's going well, home life is amazing. What more can I ask for?"

"That's great, Cody!"

We sat down and watched the weather forecast. I snarled.

"Every year it gets worse. I fully understand why snowbirds are snowbirds." We both chuckled.

By the time the news ended, Julie had called for Brian to set the table. When he was finished, he came into the living room to get me and Cody. I went to the dining room while Cody went into the kitchen to help Julie bring everything out.

Brian sat across from me, and Cody and Julie sat at either end. Dinner smelled delicious; this chicken recipe was one of my favorites, and Julie knew it. We all dug in, enjoying our first bites before speaking.

I savored each bite of the chicken. And the vegetables were dressed with more pepper than salt, the way we all liked them.

We chatted and caught up while we ate, Cody telling us about his job and why parking lots are so fucked up. It wasn't a big secret, but to have an engineer confirm everyone's suspicion was nice.

Brian was silent throughout dinner, even getting up and clearing the table without being asked to. When he was out of the room, I looked from Cody to Julie.

"You weren't kidding. This has to suck." I stood, picking up the bottle of wine. "Who wants more?"

In the kitchen, Brian stood over the sink, rinsing dirty dishes. He didn't look like he was paying attention and almost dropped a plate.

"Hey, kid. Why so glum?" I asked.

"Did she tell you she screamed at me?" Brian's eyes welled up with tears. I left the wine and hugged him.

"I don't know what you went through in foster care, but please know Julie didn't mean to hurt or scare you."

Brian squeezed me harder, pressing his face into my chest. We stayed that way for a long time. The water ran in the background.

"I know," he said as he rubbed his nose and pulled away. "But I don't know how else to feel. And I don't know how to tell her that."

I stroked his cheek. "It's okay, Bri. How about you tell me what happened that you even sent that email at all?"

"Stupid math homework," he grumbled and went back to rinsing dishes in lukewarm water.

I nodded and waited for him to continue. He didn't. I picked the wine bottle back up.

"Look, math sucks, I know. I hate it too. Sadly, we can't let it beat us. Do you think a tutor might help?"

"Yeah, I guess." He shut the water off and took the pie from the fridge.

"I'll talk to your mom." I smiled at him. "It'll be okay. Promise."

Together, we walked back into the dining room. Brian set the pie on the table, then walked back into the kitchen for plates, a knife, and forks.

Julie shot me a concerned look. I smiled and winked at her and poured her more wine. She visibly relaxed and took a sip.

The rest of the evening was perfect. While Julie and Cody were loading the dishwasher, Brian and I sat out back on the patio and talked more.

"Do you feel angry a lot?"

"Sort of? I don't know. I don't think it's a lot…" Brian looked out over the yard.

I studied him, trying to figure out if he was lying to me. If he was, he was gifted at hiding it. He looked over at me, his eyes clear.

"I get mad about the other kids in the houses I lived in making fun of me for liking to read. Like, flashbacks and then I get mad, if that makes sense. But I'm not scared of mom…I got scared of her when she screamed…in my head, I went back to the one house where Donna screamed at me all the time…" Brian started to sniffle and dropped his head. He cried, tears dropping from his face like rain.

I pulled him close and let him work it out.

"It's okay. She won't hurt you. Julie loves you. Shh," I whispered as I rocked him.

He cried a few minutes more and pulled back, wiping his eyes.

"I know. It just brought back really bad memories. And the math homework was so hard and when I asked for help it didn't work, and I just…I lost it, " Brian sniffed.

"It's okay. You didn't mean the things you said. Did you? I do think you should tell Julie, though. She feels awful about the whole thing," I said.

"Can you help me? Tell her, I mean." He had hope in his eyes.

"Of course, I will!" I hugged him. "Brian, can I ask you something before we do?"

"What's up?"

"Do you have any other negative feelings often?"

"No?"

"At other people? Do you feel like you need to hit someone or worse?"

"No. I get sad and scared and lonely. Brit, why are you asking me this stuff?"

"I'm trying to help you, is all. If you want to talk to someone regularly, we can make that happen. There's no shame in it."

"Can I think about it?"

"Sure can. Now, come on," I said as I stood, "let's go in."

Brian stood and I held the door open for him. He led and held my hand when he stopped in the living room.

"Mom? Dad? I want to tell you..." He looked up at me. I nodded.

Brian told them exactly what he'd just told me. Julie cried, and she and Cody hugged him. As happy as I was that Brian wasn't feeling violent, I was also relieved. Teaching him how to keep it concealed was something I just didn't have the mental capacity for right now.

Julie excused Brian to his room. He stopped to hug me again on the way. When he left, I hugged Cody.

"Alright, I'm out. I'm beat."

"I'll walk you to the door," Julie said and stood up.

I took my purse off the doorknob it hung from as I walked the few feet. Julie opened the door and hugged me.

"Thanks again."

"Stop thanking me. Are you feeling better?"

"So much!"

"Good. Let you know when I'm home."

I turned and walked to my Jeep. I checked the mirrors and pulled out onto the road.

My phone chimed again.

Seventeen

I WAITED UNTIL I hit a red light to check it. It was a long and painful five minutes.

As soon as I stopped, I reached for my purse. I jabbed my hand in and yanked the phone out. I pushed the home button and scanned.

Duh! It's Shae. You okay? Ohhhh shit. Yeah, uh, after we talked I got a new number.

Fuck! She had me scared and wondering if I'd have to deal with another stalker. Could I still pin the death of this sheep on Michael? I could if I successfully talked her into reporting the call.

Good! Did you report the call?

I hated to wait until I got home, but talking to my phone to text sucked; it always translated wrong. I was only a few blocks away anyway.

I drove as fast as the speed limit and traffic allowed. I pulled into the driveway and had barely come to a full stop before shifting into park and shutting my Jeep off.

In the house, I pulled my phone back out. Shae had replied.

I did. I can go get a copy of it next week if I want one. I have the report number too.

Proud of you. Saving the new number. See you tomorrow.

I hit send and fed Minion. Then I poured a glass of wine and sat on my patio. I sipped and processed my thoughts. That bitch had me going for a bit there. Did she know I was at Julie's? I hadn't told her I was going there. She had best not be following me, or I will fuck her up *before* I kill her. What the actual fuck!

I took a swig and made a face; wine should never be chugged or swigged like that. I set the glass down, still making faces, and stared off into the distance. It was dark and the stars were out. I couldn't see them because of all the lights around. I started to drift back into my mind, this time imagining the fear on Shae's face. The recognition in her eyes when I told her why I was killing her.

What was my reason? I sat up, disturbed by that simple question. It was frustrating for me to plan a kill and not have a reason this far along. Then again, those Asian twats had it coming from the second I ran into them. But my why and how revealed themselves at the same time, like they did with most everyone else. The where was always tricky, but I'd managed to nail that every time.

I went inside and locked the door. I poured more wine and sat on the couch, pressed play on the internet TV I subscribed to, and scrolled to one of the cooking shows. A savory-type recipe was in order.

I lost count of how many episodes I'd watched, mainly because I was dozing off. When I looked at my watch, it read 11:47 p.m. So much for going to bed early tonight.

I rambled up the stairs half asleep and into my bed. I didn't bother to change or take my makeup off. Once I was comfortable under the covers, I fell asleep in seconds.

• • • • ● • ● • • •

Friday. The day I would finally figure out my why.

I threw the covers off myself and glided out of bed. I was excited but tired. Besides, I didn't see the point of dancing around. I did need to jog, though. To clear my head. To feel good and stay in shape.

The year was getting close to peak humidity. My skin wore a thick coating of sweat and sticky salt air. It felt like it was weighing me down. I pushed harder. I needed to be able to focus on nothing but Shae and finding my why at lunch. Then I could figure out the where. I had an idea but needed to go for a drive to finish researching the plan. And my kill knife would take seven or so weeks to get here, which gave me the perfect amount of time.

The hot shower felt good, and the bathroom was foggy when I got out. Opening a window would be pointless, so I turned the fan on. I couldn't even do much with my hair, and wearing a top with sleeves would make me need another shower by noon.

I wiped the water from the mirror and looked in. Visions of Shae taped to a table, begging for her life, danced across the glass. I smiled and finished getting ready for work.

Traffic didn't bug me like it would if I was headed to kill someone. I was driving to my office and not looking forward to wearing my sweater, but it was necessary. I only really wore it anymore for meetings with clients, but today it would be needed elsewhere.

Barb was there waiting for me. This was her new normal, and I appreciated it. To come in earlier than her start time just to prepare for her day was helping Barb grow in her position.

When she saw my tattoos, her jaw dropped.

"Oh wow! Those are impressive!" She squealed as she came over to look at my arms. She picked up my left arm, twisting and turning it to see all the poppy flowers. "The color is so bright! Did it hurt?"

"Not really," I said, taking my left arm and showing her my right arm and pointing. The face of death on my triceps grinned. "That one hurt. Like hell. But I love how it came out!"

Barb ran her index and middle fingers down it. "She's dressed like Morticia! And the blackish purple is…wow! Britney, these are amazing!"

"Thanks! I like 'em. Maybe one day I'll show you the giant butterfly on my back too." I smirked and turned back toward my office.

Just inside the door, I had a rack where my sweater and a couple jackets hung. The air conditioning had been set to seventy overnight, but it was chilly. I pulled the sweater off the rack and slipped it on as I shivered and sat down. I'd be done everything I had laid out before lunch after factoring in the time I'd be in a meeting. Then I could spend the afternoon looking up maps of Alligator Alley.

I picked up my phone and texted Shae. *Burgers? I'm in the mood for grease.*

I'm down!

Cool. Meet me at that Philly place in Carrollwood. They have great burgers. Noonish?

Perfect! I'll be there.

The first few hours flew. The meeting went well; I brought the new client on board and that was that. He'd mentioned that he knew Dr. Osten but was recommended by that guy, Jim, that Barb was dating. I'd have to send him a finder's fee. I finished my work and left to meet Shae for lunch.

She'd gotten there before me. I noticed the same red Kia with the white paper tag. I didn't remember paying attention to the plate last night. I was slipping again.

"FUCK!" I screamed and stomped a foot. I wanted to kick Shae's car; I wanted to kick Shae. It was her fault I didn't pay attention last night. If I didn't want to kill her…I'd want to kill someone else.

I hung my head when I admitted that it was my own stupid fault. There wasn't an excuse. I'd let too much crawl into my brain and cloud it. It stopped right now.

I fixed my face and forced the anger away, then walked into the restaurant. Shae was sitting at a table, sipping a root beer from the bottle. She brightened when she saw me.

"Britney! Come sit!" She waved me over. I stopped to grab a bottle of soda for myself first. This fucking cunt…

The place was small, designed mainly for take-out and delivery. The eating area consisted of three or four tables against a counter attached to the wall. In the front, there was another counter against the window with chairs there too. A view of traffic driving by was the best conversation topic while eating. The place had been remodeled since the last time I'd been there. It was lighter and looked bigger.

Shae stood to hug me as I joined her.

"I'm ready to order when you are," I told her as I sat down. I fought back a growl.

"Cool, me too. So what's up? Anything good since you came over Wednesday?"

"Nah." I took a drink of soda. "Just work stuff. Have you heard from Heather?" My face must have been believable because Shae's expression didn't change.

"No. I thought you said you were gonna call her," Shae reminded me. Double fuck-fucking-fuck. Though I really *did* have more on my mind than calling her. She must have not wanted anything more to do with us since she hasn't said anything to any of us.

I pulled out my phone as the server came to take our order. We gave her our choices, and when she walked away, I called Heather. She didn't answer, so I hung up.

"Nope, not leaving a message." I put my phone away and returned my focus to Shae. "What made you get a new number?"

"You did. I didn't understand how stupid it sounded for me to have given him the last one until you said it out loud." She let out an uncomfortable giggle. "I haven't heard from him since and if he'd found me, I don't know it."

"What does that mean? You're gonna wait for him to come looking?"

"Oh God, no! I'm just saying that he hasn't, and if he has, *I* haven't noticed."

It was starting to click that Shae took a lot for granted. There wasn't much else to learn about Michael that would benefit me, but I still needed to learn my why.

"What's with the car? I thought you preferred to rent nice ones instead of buy new?"

The server brought our food and set it in front of us. We thanked her and continued our conversation while we ate.

"My beater finally died. It's easier for me to have one at all times than to constantly rent one. Money isn't an issue." She was flippant about money. That set me off but wasn't a good enough reason to kill her. If she'd, say, fucked me out of my money? I'd kill her. Or at least I'd think about it. She took being able to afford to live comfortably for granted. Did she appreciate anything?

I was hungry. I dug into my burger after putting the tomato and onion on top. I bit into it, and my mouth watered even more than it already was.

Then something clicked in my brain.

Eighteen

MY WHY HAD BEEN discovered.

Every time I'd been around Shae, I'd been hungry. I even felt it when she brought up wanting to be eaten after she died. I found it strange, but my brain urged that it was true. Did that make me a cannibal or curious?

"So, what are your plans later?" I managed to ask while chewing.

The stalking would begin as soon as I had an idea of what her free time looked like. For the most part, I knew she stayed home unless one of us invited her along. I started to doubt that, though, given that she'd gone and bought a new car.

"Nothing, just sitting around at home. I like having nothing to do, actually." She was eating her fries, having inhaled her burger. "I'm sure it sounds strange to someone like you."

"Someone like me? What does that mean?" I giggled. She was really pushing my buttons. It was hard to not slap the shit out of her.

"I didn't mean anything by it! I swear! I just meant that you're more high society than me." Shae looked saddened by the thought that she'd offended me.

"Oh"—I took a sip of soda—"well, I don't really know about that. I mean, yeah, I go to nice parties and all that, but high society? I think I'm too low key and chill, don't you?"

"Yeah, but honestly, I really thought you were one of those laid-back upper-class people." She blushed.

"Thanks. That's a good thing to know. If I want to turn someone off, I only have to dress down." I smirked and finished my lunch. Shaelyn White, soon-to-be dead girl, had given me insight about how people perceive me. I could use this to my advantage.

Shae looked at the clock on the wall above the counter. "Shit, it's one o'clock. I gotta get back; I'm gonna be late."

"I'm so sorry. It's my fault for asking so many questions."

"No, no. It's not. I only wish I had more to say." Shae smiled, waving the server over. "Two checks, please."

The papers were brought over a few seconds later. We handed the server cash, thanked her, and left.

We hugged before Shae got into her car. "Let's make plans for a girls' night," she said.

"You got it. I'll leave the asking the others to you."

"You sure? I feel like they don't like me."

"They don't know you well enough. Just send a message in the group text. It's fine."

We separated and I walked to my Jeep. I knew Kristen thought Shae was hiding something. And she was. Shae was hiding that she wanted to be eaten. Not cremated or buried; eaten. That was some weird shit.

I was late getting back to the office, making me glad I didn't have any appointments this afternoon. If Shae had made me late, I'd have more than just one reason to kill her.

"Everything okay, Britney?" Barb asked me as I walked in.

"Yeah, everything's fine. Thanks. We just got caught up." I smiled and headed into my office. I pulled one side of my sweater off to test the air. Then I pulled the sleeve back on.

Thoughts of which part of Shae's body I would eat came and went throughout the rest of the day. I even looked up some pork recipes because I'd read that human meat tastes similar. Information on what organs tasted like was sketchy, so I went with a Cuban roast pork leg recipe for Shae's thigh. Those were the meatiest part of her exceedingly thin body anyway.

When the day was over, I took my sweater off and hung it back on the rack by the doorway. I said goodnight to Barb and walked out. There was no red Kia and no Shae waiting for me. I grumbled as I climbed into my Jeep, annoyed that I'd let that concern me at all. I was a cautious person, not a paranoid one.

I switched the satellite radio on, and there was a hard rock song that I liked, so I turned the volume up and drove out of the lot. Traffic was back to the normal rush-hour traffic; yesterday I'd missed it because I left work early. Today I was frustrated, annoyed, and excited—and the traffic just made it worse. I cursed at other drivers and beat on the steering wheel. My windows were up, so none of them heard me. And if anyone did, so what? Would they get out of their vehicle like an asshole?

An hour later, I was in my driveway. The nosey old lady across the street waved at me. I waved back and grumbled, then shut the engine off. Not wanting to talk to her, I got out as fast as I could without falling. I tried not to slam the door as I went inside my house.

I dropped my purse onto the entry table and flung my shoes onto the shelf below, startling Minion. She yawned as she glared at me.

"I'm *so* sorry, Princess." My tone was over-dramatic and I even bowed to her. She followed me into the kitchen, the whole way there asking me to feed her. I was grateful for the break from the emotional assault. I fed her and went upstairs to change. I was going for another jog.

Out on Bayshore, the sun had started to set, taking shreds of daylight away every minute. I wasn't wearing any reflective gear, so I'd have to be back home by the time there was no light left.

I jogged south first. I never went this way—always north in a sort of circle leading south, back to my house. But never straight south and into a circle back home. If someone wanted to follow me, my jogging pattern made it easy to do. Thinking about that made me angry. I pushed harder. My skin started to feel waxy. My breath labored and my chest tightened. I had to stop before I pushed myself into the emergency room. So, I turned around and slowed to a brisk walk toward home.

The humidity had gotten so oppressive, I was glad to be home. So was my skin—it felt like it would ooze right off of my muscles. I turned the air conditioning down and the bathroom fan on before starting the water. The hope was to minimize any kind of rebellion of sweat once I dried off. It worked sometimes, but today was a bowl of soup, making it a 70/30 chance of being helpful.

Still being angry didn't make anything better either. The jog had calmed me down, but not enough. Like I usually did when the feelings wouldn't stop, I turned the water to the hottest I could tolerate. Today that tolerance was exceptional. I gave the weather credit for that, refusing to believe my anger was getting the better of me. To let emotions have that kind of control over me would mean disaster. Disaster meant prison. I had no intentions of going there.

The water ran lukewarm, telling me my shower was over. I toweled off and got out. The window had fogged up on both sides. The air blew cold from the vent and the fan pulled the dense air up the best it could. It felt better in here than I expected. It was a happy surprise.

My phone rang after I'd changed into pajamas. It stopped as I picked it up to see who it was. I swiped the lock screen away and opened the missed call notification. It was Stu who'd called. I let him leave a voicemail.

I pressed play and then the speaker button.

"Brit, it's Stu. Look, I'm not calling about us this time. I know, hard to believe. But you need to know who you're hanging out with. Call me back."

I knew exactly who I hung out with. I kept them close and had known them all since we were kids. Except Shae. She was the wild card. She also told me about her ex-boyfriend. So, I knew her too. Or maybe I just knew what I needed to. Either way, I knew who I hung out with. I didn't know what Stu wanted to tell me, so I told myself I was calling him back because I needed to fake ignorance. I also missed him and wanted to hear him talk to me.

I swiped his name to return the call. It didn't even ring on my end when he answered.

"Brit! I'm sorry to call, but you need to hear this." His voice sounded a mix of excited and concerned.

"Stu, what's going on? Whose background did you decide to check?"

"Shae's. She filed a report about her ex harassing her. I've hung out with her, too, and so I looked further. She materialized two years ago!"

"I know," I replied.

"You know? How? Why?"

"If you calm down, I'll tell you." I loved that he was worried, but I also hated it. He was being overprotective.

"She told me everything. It took months to get it all out of her, but I'm the one who got her to file the report. She wasn't going to. Oh, and she's got a new cell phone number. She said he hasn't called it yet, and she hasn't seen him."

"So, what? You're her protector now?" He spat.

"Well, that was uncalled for. Shae and I are friends. She tells me things. Breathe. I'm not trying to do your job for you. Damn." I giggled in an attempt to hide my exasperation.

"Good. And I'm sorry. I didn't mean for it to come out that way. Just watch your back when you're around her, please?"

"I will," I lied. Michael was going down for Shae's disappearance. I'd made sure of that.

"Brit, I mean it. I don't want to see anything happen to you."

"Thanks, Stu. I promise I'll watch out for this guy. I'll get Shae to show me a picture so I know what he looks like. Will you promise to chill out a little? I know how to defend myself and I'm armed. You know this." I was as sympathetic as I could be with his being so overbearing and worried.

"Brit, this guy's dangerous." He sighed. "Okay, that's the last I'm saying. Talk soon."

He abruptly ended the call. That was as much for him as it was for me. He wanted to ask me to lunch or dinner and I wanted to see him too.

I put my phone on the charger and went downstairs to make something to eat. I had a craving for a chicken Caesar salad, though. And fries. I knew I didn't have all of the ingredients, like lettuce and thawed chicken, so I called the place up the street for delivery.

Then I pulled my laptop across the kitchen table and booted it up. I still had some maps to look at and a recipe to print. I sat down and got to work.

The recipe was bookmarked, making printing easy. So I got back to work studying maps. I was looking for buildings close to each other; proximity would be key to where killing Shae took place. Dinner arrived while I was still searching. I took a break to eat and got back to it. Two hours later, I'd found an isolated building. It was miles from anything.

And perfect for me.

Nineteen

THE NEXT WEEK AND change grated on my nerves. I was impatient again, but this time for a reason I wasn't thrilled with. I wanted Stu to stop worrying. But I also knew that if we *did* get together as a couple, he'd always worry. As would I about him. It would just get worse. So I told myself to accept the facts and did my thing.

Tonight at 9 p.m. I'd begin the first of many nights sitting outside of Shae's rented townhouse. I hadn't thought to scope out where I could park the night I'd been there, so I'd have to figure that out as I went. I remembered the road being narrow with cars lining each side. I never bothered to check for open spaces because I was able to park in her driveway that night.

"Damn," I muttered as I changed clothes and put a ball cap on. I have to drive through first and see what was what.

I checked myself in the mirror, hoping I wasn't too creepy or recognizable. Then I opened the safe in my closet to take out a few things. I needed to be prepared in case parking further away was the only option. I looked at the empty space I'd designated for my new kill knife and smiled. I was excited for its delivery. Then I grabbed the bag and opened it. There was already some duct tape and contractor bags inside. I smirked and pulled the binoculars off the shelf. I placed them in the bag and scanned inside the safe again. There was nothing else I thought I'd need, so I closed it and left the room.

Downstairs, I set the bag on the kitchen table and prepped snacks and water for the night. As I bagged some trail mix, I checked the clock on the stove. It read 8:49 p.m. It was time to leave. Not that I'd made a schedule that I had to stick to, but I did prefer to watch around certain times. It helped me to get a better understanding of what my prey did with their lives.

I placed the snacks in the bag and carried the water bottle. There was a case of plastic bottles in the back of my Jeep if I needed more. Though I frequently tried not to have to jump out and risk being seen.

I paid attention to the amount of time it took me to get to Shae's neighborhood—twenty minutes, give or take. There was traffic, but not a lot. This was the ideal time of day to kidnap someone. I'd know; it's what I do.

I drove up and down the streets, trying my best to avoid being seen from Shae's house. My Jeep stood out in this neighborhood. I made a mental note to pick up something that would blend in. I could park it in the garage in Ybor. It would have to be something I could use more than just once, though. Beaters are great cars if they're fully maintained. After all, that's what helps them blend in. It would help to have a larger trunk too.

I finally found a spot at the intersection before Shae's house. There were only two roads in and out, and they met right here. It would be easy to hightail it out if necessary. This was peak paranoia for me.

"Fuck it. I've got time to stretch this out. I'll just stay a couple hours," I told myself aloud. This started a mental argument about getting good information versus practicality. I value self-preservation.

For two hours, I sat there watching Shae's house. And the neighbors' houses around me. My Jeep had been here once already. It was nighttime then, but I wondered how many people actually had seen it. She hadn't left the house, and no one arrived. I looked around once more. Seeing no one, I pulled out of my spot and drove home.

All of the feelings descended on me again, so I went to one of the hotels on the causeway. I parked and got out, walking straight for the beach. It was either risk being caught here or on a public beach. I chose here because I didn't know how often public beaches were patrolled. Besides, Stu was working tonight. If I got in trouble, he'd come to my rescue.

The sounds of the waves lapping the sand calmed me. I sat down a few feet from the water. The weight of love, anger, frustration, and excitement was too much. I closed my eyes and imagined the undertow pulling all of my emotions from me. It wrestled me until I felt like I would drown. Then it left as quickly as it showed up.

I opened my eyes and smiled. The weight was gone and so were those stupid emotions. I held no hope that this would last any longer than it would take to satiate my hunger. I couldn't even allow myself to hold onto the sliver that I wouldn't feel anything the next time I talked to Stu. Having no emotions, no matter how temporary, was good. I could get back to planning and working on patience. The monks had taught me meditation for that, but it wasn't my style. I preferred to mentally argue with myself, with the occasional shouting. It wasn't always effective, but it also didn't require me to change my ways.

However, the point of my hiatus at the monastery *was* to learn how to change my ways. If I stuck with some habits, I'd be screwed. Being impatient was more a mental thing, and the meditation was a habit. As much as I'd wanted to learn it, I hated the practice. It was dull and slow and boring.

I stayed on the beach until I caught myself nodding off. I checked my watch and saw it was after midnight, so I stood up and brushed the sand from my clothes. I stared at the moon before turning to leave. On the walk back to my Jeep, I'd kicked up enough sand to have to brush my pants off again. Then I took my shoes off and knocked the sand out. This is why I'd avoided this place. I hated sand.

I got home and watched the house diagonal from mine for signs of movement. That nosey old coot really needed to move somewhere else. Like an old people's home. Most people didn't mind her, but most people weren't me.

Seeing nothing, I got out and went into the house. The paranoia was growing, and I had no idea how to rid myself of it. I figured it couldn't have been too serious. If it was, Ben would have pointed it out. I hissed. Maybe smoking weed would help? No, I'd heard too many people say it made them tired and hungry. Some even said it caused their paranoia. I'd have to figure something else out. Really, the only real concern with getting I'd ever had was the neighbor. She couldn't age fast enough.

I took a hot bath before going to bed. I even made a cup of Earl Grey tea. Soaking in the hot water and sipping the bergamot flavor worked wonders for my mind. I relaxed for the first time in I couldn't remember how long. I didn't care what time it was; at this point, I'd accepted that I'd sleep again after finding out how acidic long pig really was. The water cooled faster than I'd have liked, but I did keep the temperature down at night.

I drained the tub and started to dry off. Minion had come up at some point—my mind was so relaxed I hadn't noticed—and started playing with the towel as I moved it around. I hung it back up, pissing The Princess off in the process, and dressed for bed. I rinsed out my mug and set it next to the sink as a reminder to take it downstairs in the morning. Minion followed me to bed and curled up next to me as I closed my eyes.

Twenty

FIVE WEEKS REMAINED UNTIL the anticipated ship date of my kill knife. I wasn't terribly impatient now; that bath really did help. I'd thought to try a bath again, but also realized there would come a point in time when that would stop working. As I waited, though, I kept checking the emailed order confirmation and the photo I'd saved of how it was supposed to look. The colors were black and battleship gray. The pattern looked like a cross between camouflage and swirls. The handle I'd chosen was called Buckeye Burlwood, a black and whitish gold sort of swirl-patterned wood. It was beautiful. I'd appreciate that beauty more when I got to hold it in my hands.

I hadn't been out to watch Shae again in a few days, but I had plenty of days left to do that. She'd asked about a girl's night when I last saw her, but never sent a message in the group text. Instead of wondering, I texted her to find out if she was still alive. I'd hunt Michael down if she wasn't.

Hey girl! What happened to girls' night?

A few minutes passed and my phone chimed. *Oh shit! I totally spaced! Sending now!*

So you're okay? Nothing crazy you need to tell me about?

Nope. I still haven't heard from Michael. No news is good news.

I nodded; she wasn't wrong. *Good.*

I didn't say more than that because I didn't need to. The only messages I'd need to respond to now were those about girls' night.

The group text went on for sixteen minutes. It ended with us deciding to meet tonight at 7 p.m. I sent Stu a message letting him know too. I had a weird feeling; one I couldn't describe, even to myself. It was a mix of fear and instinct. Either something bad was going to happen or I really was losing it.

Is this an invite? Stu responded.

No. I just wanted to let you know where I'll be.

Why?

Weird feeling is all. I'm not feeling like myself today and just wanted you to know.

Okay, weirdo.

He was right. I was acting weird and I didn't know why. Then I got an idea and texted Shae again.

Wanna ride together? I can come get you and we'll go in my Jeep.

Me like!

Cool, pick you up at 6:30.

I tossed my phone onto the coffee table and went back to my research. Since I hadn't watched her in so long, I searched for images of Shae's neighborhood at night. I didn't find any but that was okay. I would only call my hacker friend if it was necessary. This situation didn't call for *that* level of necessary.

I had an hour left before I had to get ready, so I called Osten.

"Hey, Joe! How are you?" I'd planned to ask him about tools of his trade when it got closer to the KKD of Shae, but now was as good a time as any.

"I'm well, you?"

"Great! How are you feeling? How's Marsha?"

"All well. When can you fit me into your schedule, Miss C.E.O.?" he sarcastically asked.

"Let me ask my assistant, and I'll get back to you." I joked. We both laughed. "I think next weekend looks good for lunch."

"You got it. What else is going on?"

"I actually had a question for you. My curiosity is getting the best of me, and I haven't found much on the internet. More like I found nothing. Anyway, what use would a plastic surgeon have for a bone saw?"

"What? Why?" Osten was in shock.

"Didn't mean to freak you out or anything. I was watching a show from ten years ago, and the plastic surgeons had bone saws. I wasn't sure if it was fiction or real. Like I said, my curiosity got to me." I tried to sound like I wasn't asking to borrow one if he had it.

"Oh! You're talking about that drama show, aren't you? Nip something."

"I am. They had one, and I was wondering why it would be needed. Do you have one?"

"Well, yes, but it's not for any real reason other than I wanted it. I imagine it was in the show to add some level of gross or dramatic flair."

That did it; I knew he had one I could borrow. My plan was becoming reality.

Joe cleared his throat. "Brit, is this really just curiosity? Are you alright? I hope you're not considering any kind of plastic surgery..."

I cackled. "No! I like myself just the way I am." That was a lie. I needed to control these emotions somehow. "I'm honestly just curious. I'd love to come watch a surgery sometime if you'll let me." I didn't even try to sound convincing. He would or he wouldn't allow it. I'd get my hands on that saw regardless.

A sigh of relief came from the phone. "Good. I was going to have you psychiatrically evaluated!" Joe chuckled. "But let me think about it."

"Of course. I understand if you say no." My tone was pleasant. I really didn't care one way or the other. I had a copy of the key and knew the alarm code.

"Was that all, Brit?"

"Yeah, I think we covered everything. Lunch and my curiosity. Yep. That was all of it."

"Okay. Talk to you later. I'm headed to the lounge after dinner."

"You better not be smoking cigars!" I scolded.

"I'm not, calm down. I like the smell, and they have a decent cocktail selection. I appreciate your concern, dear." That was the best form of gratitude Joe would express for my parenting him. He'd grown weary of it, for sure. But it was reciprocal, so he knew I wouldn't stop.

"You're welcome. I've got to get ready for girls' night anyway. Talk to you later," I said and hung up.

I plugged my phone in to charge and went up to shower and change. The plumbing was weird, and I had to run the water a bit to get it warm. I started the water and opened the closet, knowing what I wanted to wear. I took out a dressy red tank top and skinny jeans. I loved this outfit because I could pull it off with sneakers or heels.

Enough time had passed that the water would be hot, so I disrobed and got in. I shrieked and jumped back from the spray. "Too soon!" Seconds later, it was the correct temperature. I relaxed, my goosebumps diminishing. *Oops.*

I didn't bother to wash my hair because I didn't want to deal with drying it. I shut the water off and dried my body. It was nice not having to towel dry my hair first then blow-dry it. The nice feeling was made better by knowing I could simply put my hair in a ponytail or leave it down with little fuss. I clearly underappreciated simplicity.

Minion came up to judge me as I got dressed and put makeup on.

"Just because you're cute at all times doesn't make you better than me," I said to her.

She just continued to stare and judge as I finished getting ready.

When I was done, I checked my watch. I had twenty-eight minutes until I had to be at Shae's. That meant I could spend a little extra time with her. I would ask her to show me photos of Michael. I didn't care what he looked like. I wasn't sure I even needed to know at all. But I'd promised Stu I'd know the man's description. And I didn't want to have it wrong when it came time to throw him under the bus. Accuracy mattered.

I grabbed my keys and purse, threw sneakers on, and headed for the door. Then I remembered I'd planned to stay the night at Shae's, and I added a little more food to Minion's bowl. I always had a change of clothes in the Jeep, so that was that. I walked outside and to my Jeep.

Tonight would be the last sleepover Shae would ever have.

Twenty-One

I PULLED UP TO Shae's house around 6:20 p.m. Her car was in the driveway, so I parked two houses down on the street. There was a silver Ford Focus sitting in front of me. It was running, and a dark-haired man sat in the driver's seat. I noticed he had a white t-shirt on, but that was all I could see of his clothing. He was alone, which looked a little suspicious. But I shook it off because I didn't know any of her neighbors or their cars.

I walked by pretending not to notice. When I reached the bottom of Shae's driveway, the silver four-door sped past, heading out of the neighborhood. I shook my head. It was weird, but I managed to let it go.

Shae met me at the door. Had *she* been watching *me*? That was even weirder than the guy in the car. At least I could tell myself that was just a neighbor going out for the night. I mean, I knew Shae was strange, but this seemed like a new level.

"Hey!" Shae greeted, flinging her arms around me. "I heard a car and thought it might be you. Come in!"

"I had to park a couple houses down, so I don't think it was me you heard. One of your neighbors just left though. Might have been him," I suggested. I walked in, closing the door behind me, and followed Twed Shae to the living room.

Shae rambled on about getting ready, and I tuned her out, choosing to think about that guy in the Focus. I was usually pretty observant and noticed more things about a person. There wasn't anything special about the Focus other than color and body. The windows weren't tinted. I wasn't able to see the interior very well either. It was dark outside, and I would have had to squat or bend over a little to get a better view. That would have been creepy as hell. Plus, if it was a neighbor, I'd not only blow my chances of kidnapping Shae from here, but also any hope of not being noticed as I stalked her.

Shae's voice broke into my thoughts.

"Brit! You okay?"

"Huh? Oh, yeah. Sorry. I was just thinking about Michael. I don't know what he looks like."

"Why do you need to know that?" Shae paled as she asked.

"Because I'm me. If he ever does show up here, I think it would be helpful." I turned to face her. "Look, you don't know if he's already here or not. No one does. He could have called from here."

"You're paranoid," she said, trying to sound calmer than she looked.

"No, I've been talking to Stu." I chuckled. "Besides, I promised you that I'd keep an eye on you. He wanted to show me a mug shot. He's just doing his job."

"I guess you're both right." She sighed and picked her phone up from the coffee table. "Let me see what I have in here."

She tapped and scrolled for what felt like forever; in reality, it was only four minutes. She was one of those people who kept everything in her phone and likely never backed it up. It didn't matter if she lost everything either. She'd be too dead to care soon.

"Here it is," she said, handing me her phone.

The photo showed her and Michael smiling. They posed, each having one arm around the other. I paid attention to him instead of her. He had dark hair and was a little tan; his skin was like a flesh-colored crayon, not almost white like mine and Shae's. He stood around five-foot-seven and had a great smile. His lips were full and a naturally reddish color. I couldn't see his eyes because he was wearing sunglasses.

I handed Shae her phone back. "Do you have any more? I can't really see his face with those aviators on."

"Oh. Yeah. Should be the next one. Scroll through. There's no nudes." She giggled. "Promise." She picked up a cup and took a gulp. She was silently freaking out.

I did as she said and found one without the aviators on. His eyes were bright green. Not hazel; actual green. Those eyes made him easy to pick out. He was an otherwise average looking guy. But pure green eyes with dark hair was a rare thing. If he was here, and if he was smart, he'd show during the day when he could hide his eyes. Or maybe he'd want her to know he was around.

Whatever they were, his plans didn't make much difference to me; I was still going to pin her disappearance on him. He'd probably go to jail for it too. If not for that, I was sure the cops had other things they could charge him with.

I handed her phone back, simultaneously reaching for the cup in her hand. Shae willingly shared it with me as she looked at the time displayed on the screen.

"We're gonna be late if we don't leave now."

"Oh! If I need to, can I crash here tonight?" I asked, standing to leave.

"Of course you can!"

"Cool, thanks. Let's go have fun." I winked at her.

We walked out her front door, Shae locking it behind us. She walked with her head down, like a sad puppy. I looked around to see if any of her neighbors were watching. By the time we got to my Jeep, I hadn't noticed anyone and neither had Shae. Still hanging her head, she climbed in.

I put the key in and turned. My Jeep came to life. Shae still did not. I shifted into drive, checked my mirrors, and pulled out. There were a handful of cars coming into the neighborhood and a few waved. *That's not good. I guess I really do need a beater.*

"Stop being mopey," I ordered.

"I'm not mopey. I'm…I don't know. But it's not mopey, dammit."

"Well, darlin', you'd best paint on a happy face then. We're almost there, and you know the girls will ask questions if your face still looks like that." I tried to be funny about it, but that's not how it came out.

"Stop that!" Shae erupted.

"Whoa! What the fuck was that?!" Had I underestimated or misunderstood this petulant child?

"Oh my God. I'm so sorry! I don't know where that came from! Britney, I'm so sorry! You almost sounded like my mom. I guess…I just lost it, I guess. I'm so, so sorry." She sounded ashamed and embarrassed.

I did my best to hide my fury. "Do NOT do that again, and don't take your frustrations out on me. I will tolerate only so much, even from those dear to me. Wanna tell me what's up with you and your mom? 'Cuz that's clearly the problem. I see why you've never brought her up before." I turned onto the road that wrapped around the mall and would take me to the valet lot by The Pub.

"Remember when I told you why I never called the feds or cops about Michael? I mentioned not talking to those I knew again as a reason? Anyway, my mom…" She turned her head and looked out the window.

I pulled into the lot where the driveway for valet was, but I stopped in a lane instead. Shae needed to get something off her chest, and now was the time. I put my blinkers on and patted her leg.

Shae's eyes misted, and she cleared her throat several times before speaking. "When I called my mom to tell her I was leaving Michael, she freaked out. I couldn't tell her why, so I just told her he'd grown cold and distant and refused to talk. I told her it had been going on over a year. She didn't care. She gave me numbers of couples' therapists and all kinds of blogs with tips." She made air quotes with her fingers as she said that. "Anyway, she lost it and told me she was disappointed in me. Basically because I wasn't about to stay miserable and terrified. See, Michael treated her well. By well, I mean he gave her a monthly allowance and bought her the house she lives in. She was so enamored with his money that how I felt didn't matter to her. I couldn't tell her the truth; she wouldn't believe me. *And* if Michael found out, he'd have killed me. She called me names and yelled at me like I was a child. She even told me I was overreacting. So I blocked her number after she hung up on me and haven't spoken to her since."

I watched the color in her face return to normal as she slowed her breathing. Her face softened and relaxed. She inhaled deeply and turned to face me.

I studied her face. It was saying that she wanted to thank me for not killing her right then.

"Feel better?" I asked, smiling softly.

"Much." She returned a smile. "Now, let's go have a good time!"

Twenty-Two

I PULLED UP ᴛᴏ the valet stand and shifted into park. Shae jumped out first. She said something I couldn't hear. I decided to wait until I reached her on the other side of my Jeep to ask her to repeat herself.

I got down and straightened my clothes. I'd started to walk, not paying attention, and walked right into something—someone—firm.

"What the shit?" I saw feet. "Oh! I'm sorry!" I looked up into Devin's face, mine revealing the shock.

"Miss Cage." He nodded. "It's alright." He wore a look of annoyance combined with apathy. He was obviously bothered by my being there.

"Really, I'm sorry," I said, trying to be disarming. It didn't work.

"It's no problem. Keys inside?" he asked, walking to the open door.

"Yes." I watched him climb up and drive off. I hadn't intended to piss him off when we were lovers; just for us to stop talking and brush it off. That wasn't hard for me. It shouldn't be any different for him.

I shrugged it off as a whatever kind of thing and walked over to a waiting Shae. She had an "uh-oh" look on her face.

"What's with the face? And what were you trying to tell me when you got out?" I asked, putting the strap of my purse over my shoulder.

She pointed at the direction my Jeep had gone. "*That's* what I was trying to say. That looked awkward."

"Not really," I cheerfully replied, taking her arm and walking toward The Pub.

"You're so full of shit," Shae said with a giggle.

I laughed and opened the door. I stepped back and bowed, inviting Shae to go inside before me. She threw her head back and cackled, then played along.

She curtsied. "Why, thank you."

I picked my head up, giggled, and followed her. The door closed behind me. The bar side on the left was loud, as were the tables to the right. We looked around for the rest of the girls; we weren't late.

"Can we look upstairs? I feel like that's where they are," Shae shouted in my ear.

"Yeah, let's do that," I yelled back over the din.

I nodded to the hostess as we walked upstairs. She hadn't even noticed we'd gone by her at all. She was too busy shouting someone's name to the line of people waiting for a table. She returned my nod and pointed to the room adjacent the top of the stairs. I smiled a thanks and walked in as we reached the top.

The girls were there, waiting for us. Danielle was the first to notice our entrance and hopped out of her seat. She rushed around to where I had set my purse down, attack-hugging me.

"You're here!" Her face lit up.

"Where else would I be?" I winked. "Let me go say hi real quick. Where are you sitting?"

Danielle pointed to the chair opposite the one I'd chosen.

"Cool. We can play footsies," I joked. Danielle shoved me playfully and went back to her seat. I walked around and hugged Sarah and Kristen. Shae did too. We all sat down and the server brought two bottles of Moscato to the table and poured us each a glass.

Danielle raised hers in toast. "To the first girls' night in I-don't-know-how-long!"

"Cheers!" The group responded and drank.

We all broke out into our own mini conversations while looking over the menu. As many times as we'd been here, we never bothered to memorize it. I'd decided on the Big Ben burger for my entree, but I thought appetizers might be in order. We could be here until the placed closed since it had been so long since we were here last.

"Are we doing apps?" I asked loud enough for everyone to hear me.

All heads emphatically shook in unison.

"Well, I'll take the beer cheese," I said and smirked.

Our server came to the table and started to introduce herself. She was almost immediately cut off.

Danielle piped up. "I've got the Naughty Chips!"

Shae and Kristen both yelled, "Spinach Dip!"

Shae looked at Kristen and said, "Jinx! You owe me a Coke!"

We all laughed. The two of them agreeing to each get one since we'd all eat it.

Sarah opted for another order of the beer cheese.

Our server nodded. "I'll get this in for you ladies. My name's Shelly, by the way. If you need anything, let me know."

We all thanked her and went back to our tiny discussions until Shae stood up. My face was the only one dressed in a loud and clear annoyance. Everyone else was curious.

She raised her glass. "To Britney and Danielle. Without either of you, I wouldn't have friends at all!"

I snorted; of course she had no friends. That's the life she chose. If only she'd realized how dangerous making *me* her friend was.

The girls raised their glasses too. Mine was last.

"Aw!" The group sounded like they were ogling kittens.

I raised my glass, faking nonchalance. That bitch had better be grateful I acted like her friend this long!

Shae sat back down, leaning on the arm of the chair. She drained her glass and poured another. Her elbow slipped off, and she looked around to see if anyone noticed. Our eyes met and I shot her a concerned look. She smiled at me and mouthed the words "I'm okay." Then she turned her eyes away to join back in the conversation. I felt like I should've asked her how much she'd had to drink before I got to her house, but I brushed it away. If she wanted to get sloppy, fine. No one else would be held responsible for her behavior. Besides, her being a mess would be much better for me.

Our appetizers arrived quicker than expected given how busy the place was. Shelly set a stack of small plates and extra napkins down in front of me.

"Thanks," I said to her. I picked up a plate for me and then offered the stack to Kristen. It went around the table until Danielle had gotten the last one.

While the plates were being passed, two helpers placed the appetizers down in the middle of the table and walked away.

Shae turned and looked at Shelly. "Thank you!"

"You're welcome. Is there anything else I can get you?" she asked the table.

We all shook our heads "no," and Shelly smiled at us. "Okay, I'll be back in a little bit to check on you." She had started to walk away when I turned and called her name.

"Can I order a burger?" I asked.

"Sure can! Which one?" She pulled her notepad and pen from her apron and started to write.

"The Big Ben, please. Medium well." I was looking at the menu as I spoke, making sure I didn't want to customize it.

"Anything else?" Shelly asked me.

"Nope." I looked around at the group, hoping someone else would order something. They took turns speaking, and Shelly jotted it all down. She read each order back and the girls nodded their agreements.

"Before I forget, one check or split?"

"Split, please," Danielle and Kristen replied.

Shelly nodded and walked away.

We dug into the appetizers. No one spoke for a little while. We were all too busy enjoying our food. Then Shae dropped her fork on the floor and fell out of her chair when she tried to retrieve it. All heads turned to face her, and we burst into laughter. I almost choked on the pretzel I was chewing.

Shae stood back up, giggling. "That was *not* what I was trying to do." She sat back in her chair. "Five second rule!" she exclaimed and blew off the fork. We giggled and went back to munching and chatting.

By the time we'd finished our appetizers, our dinners had come out on a big tray. Shelly set it down on a folding tray stand and started handing the plates out. Kristen passed the dishes to their respective consumers. Shelly handed mine over with a word of caution.

"It's hot," she said.

I pulled myself back from her, giving room for her to set it down on the table. She carried the plate over with a rag so she wouldn't burn herself. Then she pulled away, grabbed the tray, and folded the tray stand back up. "Everyone okay?"

"Can we have a pitcher of water and two more bottles of wine?" I asked.

"Of course. Be right back," Shelly said as she walked away.

I watched her; she carried herself—and the tray and stand—like a seasoned veteran.

I smiled and turned back to my food. It looked delicious as I took hold of it with both hands and bit into it. The burger was perfection: swiss and cheddar, double stack beef, ham, fried onions, bacon, and the standard trimmings. It was heaven in my mouth and too many calories to count. I didn't care. It was too delightful to worry about small things like that.

We ate in silence until Shelly returned with the water and wine. She set the pitcher and bottles down, and we nodded our thanks. Our mouths were too full to open to speak. Shelly giggled and left.

Half of my burger finished, I poured myself a glass each of water and wine. Then I drained the glass of water. I picked at my fries and realized I'd need to take the rest of my food with me. I felt like I would burst.

The girls finished clearing their plates as I picked up the last fry my stomach could handle. Then Shae burped, causing all of our heads to turn to her once again.

She giggled. "Oops!" Then covered her mouth.

The rest of us chuckled and murmured and passed the bottles of wine until they were empty. We toasted to good friends and good food.

Then a glass shattered somewhere nearby.

Twenty-Three

KRISTEN AND DANIELLE JUMPED up to check on whoever had dropped it. I turned to see where Shae's pointing finger led. There was a male busser at the top of the stairs behind me. He'd dropped a glass he was carrying to his tray and was squatting down to clean up the mess.

Kristen checked that he was okay and not bleeding before rejoining the rest of us.

"Scared the shit out of me," she commented, picking her glass of wine up and taking a hefty swig.

"Us too," Shae said, motioning between her and me. I smirked and drank my wine.

Who was she to speak for me? Fucking gator food.

When Shelly returned to check on us, I asked for a box for my remaining dinner. Danielle did too, though for the remaining Naughty Chips appetizer she'd ordered. Her and I were the only ones who'd had any.

"Is that all?" Shelly asked. We read each other's faces.

"Yes," Danielle answered for us.

"Okay. No rush; when you're ready," Shelly said, handing me the stack of receipt holders. I thanked her and checked each paper to make sure I gave them to the right person. Shae came over for hers and snatched mine as soon as I set it down to grab my wallet.

"Asshole!" I called after her as she jogged back to her chair.

Shae took the paper from one and put it in with the other, then slid her card into the holder. "Nope. It's my turn to treat you. You've been so good to me…" She started sobbing.

I rolled my eyes. Jesus Christ, Shae. "I'm not *that* great, Shae," I joked.

Shae babbled. "You are. To me. I love you, Britney. You've been so accepting and kind." She didn't know; none of them did.

I smiled and raised my glass. "To Shae. Without her, we'd be lost for laughs!"

Shae broke into giggles, realizing my poke at her falling onto the floor. The rest of the girls giggled and toasted too.

Shelly came back, and we handed her the pleather folios. While she was away running the credit cards, we made soft plans for our next night here. Kristen, Sarah, and Danielle all had to check their family schedules. I shrugged my agreement, wondering if Shae would have to be seen here too. I could dispose of her before dinner. Then I started to realize the others might think it was insensitive to have a good time while our friend was missing. Would it be, though? We could be celebrating our friend in her absence. Yeah, that would work.

We were discussing a date three weeks from now, anyway. That made me strongly believe I'd have fed Shae's corpse to the hungry reptiles in Alligator Alley by then. My knife should be in my hands within the next couple of weeks, too, so I didn't see anything to stop me.

Shelly came back and handed us the folios containing our cards and change. "Thanks, ladies! Have a great night!"

"You too," we replied.

The girls signed their receipts as I stood to help Shae walk down the stairs to the door. This bitch really took it to heart when someone else offered to drive. If she were any more drunk, I'd have been dragging her limp body to my Jeep. She even said she'd been drinking before I showed up. What a fucking tosspot.

The girls stood, and one by one, we all hugged and said "bye." It didn't matter that we were all walking out together or that we'd be waiting for our vehicles together. We'd wave and say "bye" again, like always.

Shae walked down between me and Kristen, this way one of us could help her if she fell. Luckily, that didn't happen, and we made it downstairs and outside without incident. Shae burped a handful of times more between the restaurant and the valet line. People shot disgusted looks her way, but she paid no mind. Sober Shae would have noticed and said something. There may have been a fist fight, too, complete with cops and someone getting arrested.

I handed the attendant the ticket for my Jeep and a twenty-dollar bill. He nodded his thanks and ran over to a coworker who'd just left a Jaguar. He handed the keys off, and the driver vanished into the parking garage to retrieve my Jeep. Most of them knew me; I was a regular and tipped them well. Sometimes there was a new guy, but the kid who had just jogged off with my keys knew me. I could only hope that Devin hadn't made up some story about me to them.

Shae swayed and chatted excitedly to Sarah. Sarah rolled her eyes, her face showing its displeasure. Kristen, Danielle, and I giggled. We'd been through this treatment from drunk Shae. I found it particularly amusing, even with my going home with her. She'd pass out as soon as I got her into bed, and I'd be able to look around the rest of her house and neighborhood to gain a better sense of what I was dealing with. It would also help me decide what kind of half-dead beater car I'd be picking up next week. I'd decided to keep it in the garage in Ybor where I'd killed Alex. It was a good place, and I was grateful to still have access to it.

My Jeep pulled up and the driver jumped down.

"That's a sweet ride you've got!" He was new.

"Thanks," I said and handed him a twenty. "I like it."

I turned and gently took hold of Shae's arm. She jumped, startled, and turned to see who was touching her. She smiled thankfully when she saw it was me. Then she said "bye" to the girls again and allowed me to help her climb up and into the passenger seat. How I wanted to drop her and watch her bleed as multiple scrapes and cuts opened in her skin. I smirked on my walk around and hopped in. The keys were already in it and the air conditioning on.

I waved to my friends and pulled away. Shae's head bounced off the window, and I glanced over. She was out cold. I smirked and turned the radio up.

On the way back into Shae's neighborhood, I took stock of the types of cars lining the street and in driveways. Most were sensible, like Hondas and Toyotas. Others were BMWs or Mercedes. The majority, though, were the affordable Japanese kind. That meant I'd only spend a few hundred dollars and be set. I'd check Craigslist and get something from a private owner and pay cash. The registration would have to be in my name or my company's; I'd easily be able to explain why I was here.

Then I began to wonder. Did I even need a beater? I mean, yeah, my Jeep has already been seen, and if I'm pinning this on Michael—

My thoughts stopped short when I noticed an open parking spot at the end of Shae's driveway. Happiness filled me, and I drove as fast as I could from the intersection half a block away. Then I noticed that same silver Focus on the opposite side of the street. The man from earlier appeared to be sitting inside again. I strained to see better, but its windows were wet. That meant the air was on and the car was running. But for how long? I shrugged it off again and vowed to come back out and check under the guise of going for a walk. If he were still out here, I'd try to get more info, like what he looked like and the tag.

First, I had to take Sleeping Dipshit inside and put her to bed.

Twenty-Four

BEFORE SHUTTING MY JEEP off, I reached over and nudged Shae. She flung her arm, trying to remove my hand. I pushed a little harder. Her face rocked on the window, smushing into it, and she left a bit of drool. That was nasty but also something I could clean myself before the detailer got ahold of it. I didn't need him having any weird questions about what was on the window. I had to stick to my plans for them to work. Plus, I was grossed out enough by it.

I shook Shae again, harder this time. She finally started to open her eyes.

"What?" she asked, groggy.

"I need you to walk into the house. I'll help you get to bed," I said, my voice calm.

"Ugh," Shae groaned. "Okay."

Her head still against the window, she started fumbling around for the door handle. I shook her one more time while saying her name.

"What!" She snapped her head up, and eyes popped open simultaneously.

"That's better," I said with a smirk. "If I didn't wake you up, you'd have fallen out face first, dumbass. Let's go inside."

She glared at me for a second then turned and let herself out. I wasn't thrilled either. Had she fallen out; I wouldn't be able to kill her on my timeline. Besides, the girl had enough damage. More would make any time remaining with her insufferable.

I opened my door as Shae dropped down to the ground. I smirked again, then glanced up the street. The Focus was still there with its fogged windows. I squinted in a sad attempt to see through the windshield but saw nothing more than a shadow. Soon I'd get a better glimpse.

Shae walked around my Jeep and stopped at the bottom of her driveway, catching my attention. Her head lolled just shy of dropping altogether. I slammed my door and rushed to her side, locking and arming the Jeep as I went.

When I reached her, I wrapped my arm around her shoulders. She tried to say something, but I ignored her. I was more concerned with getting her inside and into bed—and figuring out who was in that car. At the absolute least, I'd have a tag number. I could call my hacker friend to run it and pull the name of who rented it if need be. I really didn't want to call him for something this trivial, though.

Shea was leaning on me at the front door, half asleep. I nudged her, she groaned, and bobbed her head. Seeing she wasn't reaching for her keys; I stuck my hand in her purse. I fumbled around for a second or two, then pulled them out. Shae heard them jingle and tried to grab them. She missed and lurched forward, her head coming close to the door frame. I struggled to keep her steady and unlock the door, but somehow managed.

"Where are we?" Shae slurred when she heard the lock disengage.

"Your house, babe. Come on, let's get you into your bed," I said and guided her through the entryway. We paused to close the door.

"Are you gonna lock it?"

Wow! She was a demanding drunk asshole. I turned around, not bothering to help her stay standing, and locked the door. I watched her sway as I turned the lock, hoping she might fall. She didn't.

I wrapped my arm under hers, linking elbows. Shae led the way upstairs with her eyes looking like slits. At the top was a small hallway that led to the left. The door on the right was a bathroom. The door at the end of the hall was a bedroom. Shae turned left into her bedroom. It was a decent size and had an attached bathroom. The walls were dark gray, accented by bright white door and window trims. The bathroom door was open enough to see part of the sink and the white wall it was attached to. That must have been blinding on a hangover morning. I'd probably find out tomorrow.

The bed was a mess of white blankets and pillows. I'd be lying if I said I didn't expect the mess. However, I was caught off guard by the plain white. I figured it was a good thing I didn't plan on killing her in her bed. That would leave a mess no landlord would be happy about. Besides, it's a townhouse; the neighbors can probably hear through the walls. If they were built like mine, though, the neighbors heard nothing.

As I helped her to the bed, she stumbled and reached out to try to grab something. I shifted to help her regain her balance.

"Thanks, Michael," she murmured.

Interesting. He'd help her after he'd beat her. What a fucking piece of trash. I actually felt my plans were justified. I didn't do the vigilante justice thing, though it did make my life easier.

Shae plopped onto the bed, fully dressed and shoes still on. I sat on the bed next to her and took her shoes off. Then I stood and covered her.

"I'll be right back. I'm getting you a glass of water," I told her.

"There's a glass in the bathroom. I leave one up here."

I went into the bathroom and filled the glass. The door should have been closed; it was a mess of hair and dirt and soap scum. I shivered and my skin crawled. How did she only keep half of this house clean? Her being this gross could have been my reason had I known before now. I was already committed, but I added this to the list of things that irritate me about the woman.

She was snoring by the time I set the glass on her nightstand. Perfect!

I padded as lightly as I could out of the room and down the stairs. I fussed with her key chain and slid the one for the lock on the front door off. There were two other keys: a car key and another one that looked like the one I'd just taken off. But this one had a pink rubber thing around it. I decided I'd try to figure out what it opened when I came back from my walk.

I unlocked and opened the front door as noiselessly as I could. I decided to leave the lights on inside, mainly so I wouldn't trip or injure myself when I went back inside. I stepped out, looking down the driveway to the silver Focus. The windows were still fogged, but that was all I could make out from this distance. I walked out, pulling the door closed. Then I turned around and locked it. If something happened to Shae while I was babysitting her, the cops would aim for me when she went missing.

The closer to the end of the driveway I got, the better I could see into the Ford. The windows were still fogged, but it had lessened a bit. Water droplets ran down in various patterns, allowing a blurred glimpse of a human inside. I smiled and turned right at the sidewalk. The front of the Ford was facing the other direction, making it easier for me to circle around the back of it. My hope was to sneak up from behind and be able to see the guy from the side.

Staying as normal as I could, I watched the car as I walked. Once I'd gotten to the point I'd have to turn around to keep an eye on it, I walked another three-car distance. Then I banked left toward the opposite side of the street and crossed. Movement in the corner of my eye made me turn my head just a little. The driver's door of the Ford opened, and a man got out. He pushed a button and the window dropped about six inches, then he closed the door. I kept pace; slowing or increasing would make me look paranoid. I needed to see what he looked like and what he was doing.

As I stepped up onto the sidewalk, I was afforded a better view. There was a streetlight halfway between the man and me. The light reflected off his dark hair. He was wearing a light-colored t-shirt and pulling a cigarette from the pack. He placed it between his lips and lit it. The lighter flashed in front of his face, and I barely made out the color of his lips. They matched what I'd seen in a photo earlier. Keeping stride, I closed on him faster than I liked. This walk was intended to be a quick one but to also gather what I could about this man.

He exhaled smoke as I drew closer. I kicked a pebble I hadn't seen, and he jumped. So did I. He spun around, lit cigarette in hand. The light washed over his face. His green eyes sparkled.

Twenty-Five

I SMILED AND WAVED.

"So sorry! I didn't mean to scare you. Shit, I scared myself," I lied, brushing hair from my face.

He'd gotten a good look at me and returned my smile, but in a more lurid sort of way. He nodded and took a drag of his cigarette. He eyed me for another second like I was a platter to be consumed, then turned back to face Shae's house, leaning his back against the car.

This man, standing here smoking, was the exact same man Shae ran back to Tampa from. Seeing him doing what I do—watching—brought new life to my hobby. I looked at a few of the neighboring houses. Some had those doorbell cameras with the blue circle, others had the pods you knew were cameras. I didn't even need to document this myself; what Shae didn't know wouldn't hurt her. Or, at least, *he* wouldn't hurt her.

This meant more work for me though. I'd need to keep an eye on him and come up with a backup plan in case he decided to pull something. I didn't want to take the chance that he was here to kill her. That was for me to do.

If he got in my way, I could say he attacked me and that it was self-defense. It wasn't like the cops didn't know who the man was. They just didn't know he was in town. The idea was to keep it that way. I could act and tell the cops I'd seen someone once or twice outside of Shae's but thought it was just a neighbor. If it came down to it, I would kill him, but only out of necessity. I needed him on camera like this. His face was clear, and my run-in would be seen. I couldn't have set this up any better myself.

I crossed back to Shae's house and opened the door. I turned to wave to Michael before going inside. He threw his cigarette on the ground and got into the car. I giggled darkly as I closed and locked the door behind me.

The next morning, I was making coffee when I heard glass shatter followed by Shae's scream. I ran upstairs.

"FUCK!" She was on the floor, picking up wet glass.

I went to the bathroom and grabbed the first towel I saw. Then I walked over and knelt beside her, cleaning up the water. "Are you okay?"

She nodded and her face flushed. I couldn't tell if it was anger or embarrassment. "Yeah, I'm fine. I reached over for the glass and knocked it off. No big deal." Her eyes were red.

"Well, I started coffee. Are you hungry? I can make a greasy hangover breakfast if you want."

Shae's face lit up. "That would be amazing! Ouch," she said, grabbing her forehead.

I chuckled. "Did you not expect this?" I finished wiping up the water at the same time Shae picked up the last piece of glass. I reached a towel-covered hand for the glass, which she gladly passed over, and stood.

"Thanks, Brit," Shae said, also standing. "I'm gonna take something and wash my face. Be down in a few."

"Okay. I'll start breakfast." There was an evilness inside my smile. I walked downstairs, dumped the glass into the trash, and threw the towel onto the kitchen table. She could move it when she came down since I didn't know where the washing machine was.

I washed my hands, then searched the meager contents of the fridge for a suitable hangover cure. I found bacon, sausage, eggs, and cheese. This would be a good breakfast.

Her pots and pans were old and falling apart. She didn't use them often either. I washed them to get the thin layer of gook off, then dried them. As I started cooking, I heard Shae stumbling around upstairs. I cackled. She made it too easy not to.

A door slammed followed by a thump. Shae cursed on her way down the stairs. My eyes were wet from stifling my laughter as I kept my face trained on the hot pans.

"Fuck, that hurt," Shae said, rubbing her arm and looking for a coffee mug.

"What happened?"

She took a mug from the cabinet, poured herself some coffee and refreshed mine. "I walked into the door frame," she grumbled. "Twice."

I giggled. "Thanks for the refill." I nodded at her, took a sip, and then took the pot of eggs off the stove. Everything was almost finished.

I set a plate of bacon on the counter in front of Shae. She took two pieces and shoved them into her mouth, moaning in delight. The grease must have been helping because she perked up a little. I munched on a piece as I pulled the last pan of bacon from the oven and turned the burner off under the pan of sausage. I plated everything except the eggs.

Shae pulled plates down and sat one next to her, nodding at me. Then she took the pot of eggs and poured more than half the contents onto her plate. As I joined her, I placed the filled plates down in a row between us for easier access.

We ate in glorious silence. I wasn't sure how much more time alone I could spend with her and not kill her. She's annoying and crazy. Yet I felt a pang of guilt. The woman had been through hell and here I was excited to kill her. From a logical point of view, that's what I do—I kill people. Having more feelings was a true inconvenience.

After draining mine, I poured both of us more coffee. Shae nodded her thanks, her mouth too full to speak. She cleared her plate and put it in the sink to wash later.

"I feel so much better! Thanks again, Brit." She rubbed her belly and took the rest of her coffee into the living room.

I finished my food and coffee, then followed Shae's lead. I didn't join her on the couch though.

Instead, I picked up my purse and slung it over my shoulder. "Minion needs food. I've gotta go home." Then I sniffed my breath from a cupped hand and made a face. "And I really need to brush my teeth."

Shae stood and hugged me. "Do this again soon?"

"Sure," I replied with a smile. I unlocked the door and left.

There was no silver Ford Focus outside that I could see. I smirked and walked down to my Jeep. My plan was taking shape nicely.

Twenty-Six

WHEN I GOT HOME, my nosey neighbor was picking her newspaper up in her driveway. She waved as she stood. I waved back after shifting into park. She walked back up her driveway and into her house, leaving me alone for the moment. I figured if I didn't say anything to her, she'd leave me alone until I got into my house. Or maybe I was just being paranoid again. It was around the same time she grabbed her paper every day. I shook my head and went inside.

I took my shoes off and set them on the stairs to take them back up and into my closet. I hung my purse on the rack and walked into the kitchen to feed Minion. She wasn't anywhere I could see her, so I called for her. By the time I pulled her food container out of the cabinet, she still hadn't come down.

"What is going on?" I asked aloud. Then I went upstairs, taking my shoes up with me.

Minion was sprawled out on my bed. She heard me and turned her little head to face me. I put my shoes away and petted her before picking her up, totally against her wishes.

"Oh stop, drama queen. Are you hungry? Come on, let's get you some food," I said to her and put her down on the floor. She stretched and yawned, glaring at me for my insolence. I chuckled and went back downstairs. Minion padded right behind me.

When she was happily scarfing her food, I started my day. Sundays were for laundry and cleaning. And that's how I spent most of the morning and early afternoon.

I showered after I was finished cleaning and put the clean clothes away. Then I plopped down onto the couch and turned streaming on. I scrolled to a documentary about cannibalism and pressed the play button.

Three hours later and I'd learned only a small bit more than even fiction had told me. Ritualistic and survivalist were the main reasons for it. Yet Dahmer admitted to eating his victims. Not for the same reason I planned to, but more to keep them with him. At least, that's my belief. Psychology says it was more of a power trip kind of thing. Whatever his actual reasons, he never told anyone who then shared it with the world. Not that I could find, anyway.

It didn't matter. My reason was much simpler; Shae expressed a desire to be eaten after death. She never specified a species or animal she wanted to feed, just that she wanted to be food instead of cremated or buried. I could handle that. On top of that, I was curious what human meat tasted like. It was rumored that gators already knew, making them more a disposal method than having a need to feed them.

My stomach made a noise. I was hungry now just thinking about eating Shae. I chose to actively stop myself from thinking about it until Shae was dead and under Osten's bone saw. I picked my phone up from the table and opened the delivery app.

Thirty minutes later, the tacos I'd ordered showed up. I thanked the driver and used the app to tip him. Then I took my food into the kitchen and sat at the table to eat.

While I ate, I mentally ran through some key details of my planning. At this stage, I still needed to follow Shae some more, if only to verify that she truly had no social life outside of our small group. I also had to borrow Osten's bone saw. From there, I'd drug and kidnap Shae. Then she'd die. Voila! The end.

My phone rang as I swallowed my last bite. It was Osten.

"Hey, Joe!"

"Hi, Britney! I've been thinking about you observing during surgery. I've got a glass wall that was intended for this purpose, but never used it since I don't teach. You can watch from the observing room. Anything more would open up all kinds of sanitary and legal issues. I hope that works for you."

I nearly squealed. "That's perfect! Thanks, Joe! I didn't know you wanted to teach," I commented.

"I did. Then I had my heart attack. I wanted to tell you about it before now, but it never really came up," he said.

"That's really cool of you. To want to teach and to let me observe, I mean. I wish you hadn't had the heart attack, but I'm glad you learned how to slow down." I hissed when I sucked my breath in. "That didn't come out right."

Joe laughed. "I know what you meant. So, when can you come in?"

"I'll work my schedule around you. You're freely giving me your time in surgery; I'd be a dick to ask you to work around me."

"Okay, then. I've got a good opening in two weeks. We can grab lunch after," he replied.

"Sounds great. Text me the date and time, and I'll be there. Thanks again, Joe! Oh! Before I forget, if there's anything special I need to wear, let me know in the text. I think I'm gonna get some sleep now. It's been a long weekend."

"You got it, kid. Love you."

"Love you too," I said and hung up.

I was tired, sure. But not enough to go to bed. And now I had to run though getting into the supply room that kept his tools. Things were falling into place so perfectly.

Twenty-Seven

FOR THE NEXT TWO weeks, I sat outside Shae's house at various times throughout the night. One night would run 10 p.m. until 1 a.m., another would be 11 p.m. until 2 a.m. And a few other weird schedules too.

I chose this kind of randomness for a few reasons, the first being Michael. He was there every night and left before I did. I'd chosen not to get a beater car because the neighbors knew my Jeep anyway. I did, however, notice which houses didn't have any sort of cameras. I parked in front of those houses when I could, which was most of the time. Michael parked in the same spot I'd seen him in the night I saw his face. He was making this too easy.

The more time went by, the less concerned I was that he'd kill Shae before I could. If he'd planned on it, I'd likely interrupted those plans. I knew he could have done it already, but he didn't. It wasn't my job to wonder why. It was, however, mine to keep watching and waiting.

Each night I sat out there, I ran though different scenarios in my mind. The ones where the cops inevitably came calling and asking about Shae.

My neighborhood was part of Stu's usual beat, so they'd probably send him to talk to me. If not to talk, maybe to notify. I wasn't sure who Shae's emergency contact was, but she had all she needed to make it me. I planned accordingly. The things I couldn't control—like Stu possibly having to question me—weighed on me.

Stu and I hadn't spoken much in the past few weeks other than a few random test messages. They weren't anything substantial, either. Just a series of "hi, how are you?" kind of things. Tonight, watching Michael watch Shae, that changed.

I picked up my phone and typed.

Hey! When are we having dinner? I miss you.

I played with the satellite stations. Minutes turned into hours before I heard back from Stu.

Hey! Sorry for taking so long. I'm just finishing my shift. Does tomorrow work?

Of course. Wanna meet up or…

I'll be over at 7. Makeup not required. We're staying in.

See you then.

I put my phone back in my purse and sighed. I really did miss Stu and still wanted to be with him. He was *always* on my mind, no matter what I had going on.

I looked in the rearview mirror; Michael was still there in the Focus. And Shae was still alive. Maybe he didn't want to kill her after all. I didn't know. What I did know was that *I* would be her killer. But first, I needed some tools. And next week, I'd have them.

I left soon after, having nothing more to watch than Michael. It would all be over soon enough.

The next day was the day I'd be borrowing Joe's bone saw under the guise of being interested in watching a surgery. I arrived at his office about twenty or so minutes early to look around. I'd seen most of the floor but not the surgery suite. I'd also never seen the room where Osten and his operating staff washed their hands. That room was the most important one of the day; the whole reason I was here.

The receptionist told me that it was okay to go back and change into scrubs. I wasn't sure if she knew I would be on the other side of the glass wall or not, but I listened to her anyway. She also said something I didn't realize I was supposed to do. That I needed to go to the locker room, and she handed me a piece of paper. On it was written a number and a combination. Did Joe spring for new lockers? I swore he had the employees bring their own locks. I thanked her and walked away.

Inside the locker room, I quickly understood why I was being assigned a locker. A sign above six lockers read "Observation Team." Joe really did want to teach, and he'd had the place totally outfitted for it. I used the combination and opened the locker to find a set of clean, cobalt blue scrubs. I knew it wasn't a shade of blue Joe had his employees wear; they all wore different colors depending on their function. I changed and put my clothes and purse inside. Then I closed the door and turned the dial to lock it. I patted the pocket on my chest to make sure I had the combination. It didn't matter if I lost it anyway. I could get it again from the receptionist.

I walked out of the locker room and to the wash-slash-supply room. All of Joe's instruments glimmered under the bright lights. They looked like they were on display at a museum or something. Each instrument had a place on each glass shelf behind glass doors. I didn't see any fingerprints anywhere. Everything was spotless and sparkling. I was positive someone's only job was to make sure things constantly glistened as though they were covered in glitter. I smiled and continued to look around.

I found the bone saw in a bottom cabinet, along with a handful of other instruments. I had no idea what the rest were and didn't care. The door of this cabinet was a light-tinted glass. I figured it was because these pieces were rarely used. I stared at the bone saw and tried to figure out how I'd get it out of here without being obvious. It was small enough to fit in my purse. Or rather, my purse was large enough to hold it. Technicalities aside, I glanced up at the clock on the wall. I only had a few minutes to go hide this thing and come back. No one was around, and I didn't see any cameras.

I noticed a box of rubber gloves and put a pair on; fingerprints would absolutely be seen. I opened the glass cabinet door and wrapped my hand around the bone saw. I smiled wryly as I pulled it out. It was much smaller than I thought it would be. I'd even done some research on them, but my brain must have made the dimensions somehow larger. I closed the cabinet door and speed walked to the locker room. I opened the locker door as quickly as I could and shoved the saw into my purse.

"Brit, you in here?" Joe called as he walked into the locker room.

"Right here! Just tying my shoes," I lied.

Joe walked over and hugged me. "Ready to go?"

"Yep! Show me the way!"

Osten led me to the observation room and kissed me on the cheek before leaving. I had to admit I was excited. Not just because I'd succeeded in grabbing the saw, but also because I *did* want to watch a surgery.

Joe walked into the surgery suite and got to work. The patient had already been put under. He was handed a shiny scalpel and began conducting his surgical symphony the second his fingers closed around the handle.

I watched for the entire hour and a half. It was so mesmerizing; I hadn't even realized the implants had taken that long. Joe nodded for me to meet him back in the locker room. I smiled, mouthed the words "thank you," and headed out.

In the locker room, I was elated as I changed. I threw the scrubs into the laundry bin and changed back into my own clothes. Joe had done the same in his private bathroom. He was walking out of his office just as I was walking to meet him.

"What did you think, kid?" He put his arm around my shoulders as we turned and walked out of the office.

"It was amazing!" I gushed.

"Glad to hear it! Now, let's eat!" Joe led the way to the garage. I patted my purse and smiled.

Twenty-Eight

BACK AT THE OFFICE, I didn't have a whole lot of work for myself or Barb, so I took the time to act like the person she thinks I am. I asked her about how she was and how things with Jim were going. Apparently, Barb had been wanting to tell me for a while now. She erupted in a flurry of speech and facial expressions when I asked.

"It's going so much better than I ever thought it would!" Barb's face turned red with excitement. "Jim's such a nice guy! He never lets me pay for anything, but I always get to pick where we go or what we do. Like, last week, we went antiquing. And Jim's not into that kind of thing, but he went because I wanted to go. He says he's enjoying getting to know me. I know I'm having a great time getting to know him!"

"That's wonderful! Have you two done anything he likes?" I asked. Jim would have quickly become a *why* if I found out he was luring my assistant for some nefarious reason.

"We have! He likes the outdoors and stuff like that. We've gone zip lining, hiking, biking, and we've got plans to go tubing! I never knew how much fun any of that was before. I was always scared of snakes and big spiders and things like that."

"I'm afraid of the same things," I chuckled. "I'm proud of you for facing them anyway. It's always good to experience new things."

"It is! Oh! Jim wanted me to thank you. Not just for placing him, but for hiring me. We never would have met otherwise." Barb blushed and smiled.

"You're both very welcome," I said. Then I lowered my tone to one more serious. "If he does anything weird or suspicious, I hope you'd tell me. You know I have friends on the force, and we can have things handled properly…"

"Oh, Britney, he would never! But thank you! It's good to know you care about me."

I was really just trying to protect my investment, but if that's how she wanted to see it, I wasn't about to tell her different.

Jim was a decent enough guy even back when I'd interviewed him, but his making everything about Barb was odd. To me, anyway. No one had ever done that for me. Sure, Stu did what he could, but it was never like what Barb described. It was honestly a concern. I'd have to keep listening and asking. Barb was a good person and employee. I'd be damned if I'd let anyone take her from me. I was growing as protective over her as those I cared about. I just pay her, and good employees are hard to find.

My phone chimed, drawing my attention while Barb answered the phone. It was a text from Stu.

Do you mind if I come over early?

I was tempted to ask why but didn't. *Sure.*

OK. See you at 6:30.

I'd be home by 5:30 p.m. I'd change and feed the cat and be somewhat bored until Stu got there. Or I'd spend the empty time watching more—no, I wouldn't. There wasn't anything more to learn from documentaries.

Barb hung up as I walked into my office.

"Oh wow! I didn't even realize the time," she said.

"Me either," I replied as I picked up my things.

I walked into the reception area and hugged Barb. "I'm glad you're happy. Please tell Jim I say hello."

"Of course!" She let go. "Have a great weekend!"

"You too." I smiled and walked out the door.

Traffic was light, and I was parked in my garage within seventeen minutes. I got out of the Jeep and walked into the house. Minion greeted me in the kitchen. I fed her and headed for the stairs, leaving my purse and shoes in their homes near the door.

Once in my room, I changed into leggings and a t-shirt. Then I opened the safe. I took out the bag I used to pack everything in and did just that. Contractor bags, duct tape, nylon rope, ketamine and syringes…

It dawned on me that I hadn't checked the front door for packages. My knife should be waiting for me. And if it wasn't here today, it should be tomorrow. I couldn't believe that I'd let the excitement fade.

I jogged down the stairs and opened the door. A brown box greeted me. I squeaked and snatched it up before slamming the door. I hugged the package and tore back up the stairs to open it.

On the floor in front of the safe, I sat down and placed the box next to me. I grabbed the utility knife from the shelf and cut the tape. In my happiness, I'd tossed the knife aside without retracting the blade, and I heard it snap. It was an easy fix, but I still rolled my eyes.

Like a kid opening gifts, I tore into the box. In it, there were those air pillow packing things around a heavily wrapped, oblong object. My excitement grew. I unrolled the paper and picked the knife up by the sheath.

The end of the handle and pommel gleamed in the light. I squeaked again and removed the sheath. The blade was perfect. The Cerakote came out even better than I'd imagined. The Battleship Grey and black swirled and twirled along the six-inch blade. The blade was sharp as it was, but I'd have to have it sharpened or do it myself. I didn't know of anywhere I could have it done, but I knew sharpeners were easy enough to get just about anywhere. I mentally noted to pick one up this weekend. Next week would be too late.

I slid the knife back into its sheath and placed it in the home I'd made for it. Then I finished packing the bag and placed it back inside the safe. I closed the door and turned the dial, smiling the whole time.

I used my knees to help me stand and looked at the clock on the wall. It was a few minutes past six, so I went downstairs and turned the news on. The weather was all I really cared about. There was a commercial on, so I went into the kitchen and grabbed a beer from the fridge. When I came back into the living room, the weather report was about to start. Perfect.

The weather ended, and I picked up the book that sat on the coffee table. It was a genre new to me, but I liked the story so far. I'd gotten a copy for Brian, too, but he was still grounded. There was no way Julie would be happy with me if I gave it to him now. So his copy sat on my bookshelf in a plastic bag so it wouldn't collect dust.

I'd barely gotten back into the flow of the story when the doorbell rang. My heart leaped with joy. I stood up, closing the book and setting it on the table. At the door, I found myself nervous. That was unusual for me in this situation. I took a deep breath, swallowed, and opened the door.

Stu bear-hugged me.

"God, I missed you!"

I stepped backwards and pulled him along with me. Stu closed the door with his foot as I pulled back to look him in the eyes. They sparkled with love and adoration. I was confident mine showed the same and kissed him.

Stu briefly kissed me back, then retracted. "As much as I enjoyed that…" He let go of me and held my hands.

"I know. I'm sorry. Can I get you anything to drink?"

"Nah, I know where your fridge is." He winked and walked off toward the kitchen. I heard Minion greet him and giggled.

I sat back down on the couch at the same time Stu came back. He joined me and we toasted.

I raised my bottle. "To us finally getting together again!"

"Hear, hear!" Stu said with a grin. We clinked and took healthy swigs before setting them back down on the coasters.

Stu pulled his phone from his pocket, snapped a photo of me, then opened a delivery app.

"What was that all about?" I asked.

"So you'll be with me at all times," he replied, smirking but not looking up from his phone.

I chuckled and leaned into him. "What are we eating?"

Stu tapped a few more times before answering me.

"It's a surprise." He set his phone on the coffee table and picked his beer back up. "So, what's going on?"

We chatted and caught up for over an hour. He told me about work and that he had taken a lot of overtime to keep himself busy. I told him I'd been spending more time with Shae, which wasn't a complete lie. He was happy to hear that, especially because he'd heard rumors that Michael was in town. I nearly spat out my beer.

"I'm sorry, what? He's here?" I was probably more dramatic than I should've been.

"I can't confirm it. It's just a bunch of former associates of his trying to rile us up, I'm sure. But still, you have to be careful. Don't tell Shae; I don't want her to freak out."

"I won't. But I don't think she'll do much freaking out. More like she'll drink herself to death."

Stu arched an eyebrow.

I told him about her drinking habit, and if she had seen Michael, she may have only been hallucinating.

"Awesome," Stu groaned. "Even if he *was* in town—"

The doorbell interrupted whatever Stu was saying. He jumped up, grinning like a fool, and opened the door. He came back with a large paper bag and headed straight for the kitchen. I picked our beers up and followed.

I wasn't far behind, but Stu had already started taking things out of the bag. On the table sat all of my favorites from my favorite Thai place. My face lit up, and I rushed to gather place settings and napkins for the two of us. I glanced at Stu and noticed he was wearing a smile of unadulterated joy and happiness. I felt the same way.

We sat down and enjoyed our dinner, making small talk and avoiding our feelings for each other. I almost let it slip about my hobby because I was still excited about receiving my knife, and I hated hiding it from the man I wanted to be with. I bit my tongue to stop myself.

After we finished, Stu cleared the table and even put the dishes in the dishwasher.

"You're a great housewife," I joked.

Stu laughed and shook his head.

We spent the rest of the night watching movies and acting like we used to before all the feelings came up. It was a wonderful night.

Around eleven, Stu stood up and stretched. "I think I'm gonna call it a night. It's been along week."

"Okay." I sighed and stood. We walked to the door and kissed "bye."

I leaned against the door with my eyes closed. I should have told him I love him. I should have told him we could be together. But I didn't. Instead, I almost lost him altogether by nearly spilling my guts. I knew that I couldn't' keep my secret much longer. Time was no friend of mine; I'd be disposing of Shae this upcoming week and then be questioned about her disappearance.

I needed to decide what I'd be telling Stu, if anything at all. Maybe waiting a while would be better? I strongly doubted that. I shook my head and locked the door, still thinking about how I felt. I turned the TV off and lumbered upstairs.

I needed to get some rest. Then I could figure out what was what.

Twenty-Nine

WEDNESDAY ARRIVED FASTER THAN expected. I was glad I was able to find a great stone and sharpen my knife in time. Today would be the day I kidnapped and killed Shae.

We'd even have lunch together. I knew I'd be the last one to see her alive; I'd kind of planned it that way. I'd be the first person questioned and probably the last too. It would drag on for hours, and I wouldn't be able to tell them much more than I'd first told them.

I played my lines though my head as I drove to meet Shae. I parked and cackled a little too loud. People walking by looked at me funny. I waved and turned my head to the passenger seat.

We met at our usual pizza place and had fun. Beers and pizza, lots of giggling. She didn't mention anything about Michael, and I wasn't asking. It was easier to play dumb that way. We hugged "bye" and went back to our jobs.

Night fell and I was ready. My kill bag was packed and already in the back of my Jeep. The ketamine-filled syringe was capped and waited for me in the center console. I locked up the house and climbed in.

I didn't see Michael or the silver Focus. My hands wrung the steering wheel until I felt a sting and looked down. I shook them out in turn, then parked in Shae's driveway. I slid the syringe up my sleeve and opened the door. As I jumped out, I looked around again, specifically for any sign of Michael. Not seeing one, I locked my Jeep and walked to the front door.

I rang the bell. Silence. I rang again. A light turned on inside and someone mumbled.

"Shae, it's me!"

The door swung open and she glared at me. "Since when do you show up unannounced?"

She walked away from the door, leaving it open. I walked in, closing it behind me.

"I wanted to make sure you were okay," I said, following her to the couch. It was clear she'd fallen asleep there.

"You could've called or texted."

"I know, but I was also thinking to take a road trip. I want you to go with me."

Shae perked up. "Play hooky, huh?" She arched an eyebrow and smirked. "I'm in. When do we leave?"

"Now."

Shae practically jumped from the couch and sped upstairs to change. It seemed she enjoyed this kind of thing. I enjoyed how easy she was to con.

The syringe felt cold against my skin. I couldn't drug then drag her. My Jeep was a little too high to lift her into. Plus, neighbors had cameras. I had adapted the plan as I walked to the door before ringing the bell.

Shae bounded back down the stairs, ready to go. She grabbed some cash but nothing else.

"That's it?" I asked.

"Yeah. I don't want to be bothered and there's plenty in here," she said, holding up the rubber-banded cash.

I shrugged and led the way out. She locked the door behind us, and we climbed into my Jeep. I flashed her a grin as I started the engine.

"This will be a road trip we'll never forget!"

"Huzzah!" Shae cheered. "Tally ho!" She extended her arm and pointed out the windshield.

I laughed and drove out of Shae's neighborhood.

Shae didn't bother to ask where we were going. Not even when I'd gotten onto I-75 southbound. Instead, she turned the radio up and rocked out.

Three hours later, I pulled onto a dirt road. It was lit by a single streetlight. The next one was on the opposite side of the street about a half mile in each direction. The frogs and other night creatures were loud enough to be heard through the closed windows. I'd turned the music down when we turned west, having never been this way at night. I needed to concentrate and wasn't terribly familiar with where the dirt road was.

Shae made noises like we were teenagers about to camp and tell ghost stories. I chuckled and kept driving until the dilapidated building came into view.

"What the fuck is that, Brit?" Shae laughed.

"I found it on Google Maps. Figured it would be a fun spot to explore," I answered as I shut the headlights and engine off.

"It *does* look like fun," Shae commented as she opened the door. Then she dropped down and took off toward the front door.

I hopped down and retrieved the bag from the back. Then I locked my Jeep and swung the bag over my shoulder and followed Shae.

The night was humid and loud. The front door was a simple piece of plywood. There had been a lock on it, but Shae picked it before I'd made it that far. I shook my head, approving of her resourcefulness. But my approval didn't last beyond that second.

I crossed the threshold to face an annoyed-looking Shae. I didn't bother to close the plywood door behind me. She'd had no time to react; I was on her too fast. I watched Shae's expressions change from annoyed to confused to horrified as I approached her. Her final expression was one of shock as I jabbed the needle into her neck.

As she dropped down, I caught and guided her to floor. When I stood, I took stock of what was around the room. Shae had already turned on an overhead light, making things a bit easier. There was a table near one corner and a utility sink in another. It wasn't the best of places, but it would work beautifully.

I placed my bag down near the table and went to work, cutting contractor bags and taping them to the floor. I cut a few more and placed them over the table. Then I pulled out some thin plastic—the self-stick kind—and placed all of it on the table.

I walked over to Shae's limp body after reaching back into my bag. She was breathing lightly. If only I'd known to drug her when I stayed there, the snoring wouldn't have been so bad. I wore what I'd just pulled out of my bag as a bracelet of sorts. I pulled at the silver roll and tore the first piece off, placing it on her mouth in case she woke up too early. Then I went about taping her ankles together. I dragged her over to the corner and hoisted her onto the table.

She woke as I finished using the self-stick plastic to tie her down to the table.

"Brit?" Her voice was raspy, and she was still spaced out a bit. "What's going on?"

I'd removed the tape from her mouth and ankles while I was securing her to the table with the plastic.

"Well, darlin', you're awake a little earlier than I'd planned, but that's okay. See, I've wanted to kill you since we met.

But I couldn't figure out why until recently. Wanna know?" I winked at her and took the knife from my bag.

"Why?" Her voice quivered and cracked.

"Because I'm hungry! *You* made me hungry."

"How?" She started to cry.

"Remember when you told me you wanted to be food after you died? Well, that made my stomach grumble. Every time I thought about it after that, my stomach grumbled. First, I thought it was disgust. But then…then I realized I wanted to eat part of you. Really, there's nothing much more fun than killing someone just because. But you gave me a reason."

While I talked with my voice, I talked with the knife too. Running it up and down her cheek, arms, and legs. She squirmed, trying to break free, but I'd wrapped her tight enough that she wasn't going anywhere.

"So-so, you-you're killing me just to eat me?"

"Yes," I replied flatly. "And I'll share with the gators too." Then I snapped.

"For weeks, I sat outside you house, watching you. For weeks, you bored me to tears—fucking TEARS! All because I was hungry. And I still am. You're a stupid, uninteresting, disappointing twat. And I've been waiting too long to say this with any kind of meaning. Goodbye, Shae. Goodbye," I said, raising the knife over her chest.

Shae's eyes burned into mine, pleading.

I plunged down; both of my hands wrapped around the grip. The knife slid easily into Shae's chest. The light in her eyes faded. Blood poured from the wound and pooled under her. I pulled the knife out, wiped it off, and slid it back into its sheath. It had performed exquisitely; I adored it.

Leaving her body on the table, I turned and pulled the borrowed bone saw from my bag. It was a beautiful tool, and it gleamed its agreement in the dim light. I plugged it into the portable battery pack I brought and went to work. It was messier than expected; I thought since her heart wasn't pumping, the blood wouldn't spray so much. Good thing I kept wipes in my Jeep.

By the time I was done, I was covered in blood. I was convinced there was more on me than the floor, which made that part of cleaning up easier. I grumbled as I cleaned, placing both arms, a whole leg, and half of the other leg into a bag. One thigh was mine. I'd even found a recipe for it. I'd left her head attached to her torso and slid it all into a bag the same way I put a pillowcase on a pillow.

I carefully picked up the bags I'd laid on the floor and threw them into yet another bag, along with the plastic, duct tape, and other scraps that needed to be trashed. Then I took that bag out to my Jeep and cleaned myself up. I changed into an old pair of jogging leggings and an old, black t-shirt. I'd drop them in the laundry when I took the bone saw back to Osten's office. I knew the colors matched his surgical staff's scrubs enough and would be washed. I placed my blood-soaked clothes into a bag and left it on the ground.

Back inside, I grabbed the bag I was keeping and carried it out to my Jeep, setting it off to the side a bit. I lined the inside with more contractor bags—on top of the tarp I kept there. Then I lifted each bag to be disposed of into the cargo area. When that was finished, I picked up the leg I was keeping and squished it into the back corner by itself. I ran back inside to make sure I hadn't left anything. Then I turned the light out and left, closing the plywood door behind me. I was able to secure the lock too.

I hopped into the driver's seat and drove around the back of the property. The dirt road still went back a way; that's another reason I'd chosen this place. Kill spot *and* disposal spot in one. I nearly swooned.

I backed up and parked near the edge of the swamp and got out. I could smell the roast cooking as I took the bags and bumped their contents into the water. There was a roiling of water, followed by what sounded like growling. Nostrils and tops of heads poked out from the murk. The floating bits were engulfed in massive gator maws in seconds. And then they were gone.

Off to the side of my Jeep, I dumped the bag of blood-soaked clothes onto the sand. Then I siphoned a small amount of gasoline from my tank and dropped it onto the pile. I lit a cheap lighter on the gasoline, and when it caught, I dropped the lighter into the burning mess. Because I'd set the fire on sand, it extinguished itself in no time. I hopped into my Jeep and headed back to Tampa.

Thirty

BEFORE GOING HOME, I stopped at Osten's office to return the saw and drop the clothes on my back into the laundry. I parked and grabbed my bag from the back, then unlocked the door.

First I went to the wash-slash-supply room. I cleaned off the saw, put gloves on, and returned it to its home in the cabinet. I washed my hands again, this time with real soap, then headed for the locker room. I opened the locker I was assigned and took out the clean, dry clothes I'd left. After changing again, I dropped the all-black outfit into the laundry and left. I locked up behind me so no one would be the wiser.

In my Jeep, I rode the high before starting it up to go home. For five minutes, I sat there, eyes closed, enjoying the tingle on my skin and the weightlessness of my mind. Then I opened my eyes, started the engine, and drove home.

A week had gone by before Shae's boss called the police. He hadn't planned to, but Danielle had insisted.

I was at my desk working when my cell phone rang.

"Hey, Danielle! What's up?"

She sounded panicked. "Have you heard from Shae recently?"

"No, why? Is everything okay? She didn't tell the boss off, did she?" I giggled.

"No. She's missing. Hasn't shown up to work in a week. We called the police to file a report, though."

"What! On no!" It was hard not to laugh; Shae's thigh was roasting in my oven.

"Shit, I have to go. They're here," Danielle said and hung up.

I set my phone down, sneered, and went back to work. Twenty minutes later, Stu walked in.

"Hey, Brit," he greeted somberly.

"Hey! I would say it's good to see you, buuut I think we know that under the circumstances—"

"You know?" Surprised, he cut me off.

"Yeah. Danielle called a little bit ago and told me she called."

"Well, it was the boss, but yeah. Anyway, they sent me here to interview you, but I recused myself."

"Oh. So, what are you doing here?"

"Letting you know that Officer Smith is going to interview you. And letting you know about Shae." Stu gave me a half-smile.

I returned it. "Thank you."

Officer Smith walked in and introduced herself. I stood to shake her hand and offered her a seat. She asked all the questions you hear when watching a cop TV show. I answered them as best as I could. Then she asked if I knew if Shae had any enemies.

"Well, she came here to escape her ex-boyfriend, Michael."

Stu came over from his spot in the doorway and spoke. "Smith, I can fill you in on all that. Is that all you needed Britney for?"

"It is." She looked at Stu and smiled. Then she stood and reached her hand out to shake. "Thank you for your time, Ms. Cage. We'll be in touch if we have further questions."

I shook back. "Of course. Anything you need, Officer."

Stu flashed me a smile and walked Officer Smith out. I sat back down and smiled. I was proud of myself for being able to pull myself back together enough to pull this off. But that didn't stop me from wanting to tell Stu. So I ran through several scenarios in my mind. None of them ended well, but I knew I'd have to tell him in some kind of planned way.

Just then, my phone chimed. I picked it up and read the text message.

Sorry about her. She just transferred from some county further south. Anyway, I told her about Michael, and she's got others helping her track him down. One of the CIs said they saw him around town.

I smirked. The CI was correct.

No worries. She was polite. I'm worried about Shae though.

I don't think we'll find her.

You think he killed her, don't you?

We can talk about this later.

Okay. Wanna come over for dinner and a movie?

Brit, you only need tell me the time.

6.

K. See you soon.

I wasn't even a blip on the investigating officer's radar. I was back.

I shimmied a little in celebration and shut down for the day. On my way out of the office, Barb stopped me.

"Is everything okay?" The concern in her voice was real.

"Yeah. One of my friends is missing. Stu thinks her gang leader ex-boyfriend may have killed her. It's sad. But I don't want to freak out without knowing what happened, you know?"

"Aw. Well, if I can help, let me know. Jim and I can hang posters or—"

"Let the cops do their jobs. Even Shae thought he might come for her and kill her. We should really leave it and only help when the cops call."

"That's scary! I agree. I'm sorry, Britney."

"Me too. Have a good night, Barb," I said and walked out the door.

On the drive home, I thought some more about how I'd tell Stu my secret. But by the time I parked, I had realized that no amount of planning could prepare me. So I sucked it up and shifted focus to dinner. What Stu didn't know wouldn't hurt him.

I opened the oven to check on the roasting leg and was blasted by the delicious smell. I closed the oven door and fed Minion before going upstairs to change.

I ran back down to the kitchen and pulled the dishes from their homes in the cabinets. There was a knock at the door.

"Come in!" I yelled, still setting the table.

Stu walked in, and I heard him close the door. "Brit? Where are you?"

"Kitchen!"

I'd just set out the wine glasses when Stu entered.

"Hey, babe! Wow! That smells great!"

I kissed his cheek. "Glad you're drooling. Should be ready in about fifteen minutes."

"Awesome!" Stu opened the fridge and pulled out a bottle of wine. He poured some into our glasses and sipped. "So, Michael *is* in town. A couple officers went to pick him up at some seedy motel in Clearwater. He's going down."

I smiled. "That's great to hear! Find Shae?" I sipped.

"No. I told you. I don't think we will."

"That sucks. I knew her enough to like her, but I'm not sad. What's that all about?"

"Shock. You'll deal on your own terms," Stu said and hugged me. I hugged him back.

We chatted about Shae and laughed while we waited the last few minutes for the roast. Then I took it out of the oven and set it on the table. The smell made us both drool.

"Is that Pernil?"

"It is! My first time making it too! Would you like to carve?" I asked, handing him the knife.

Stu carved and set chunks on both of our plates. We ate in mostly silence; there were random groans and moans of pleasure and enjoyment while we chewed.

After dinner, Stu helped me clean up, and we tried to watch a movie. I ruined that. And a whole lot more.

"Stu," I said, not paying attention to the screen as he flipped through looking for something to watch. "I have to tell you something."

He set the remote down. "What's up?"

I couldn't control my face, as usual, and Stu's face flushed. "I killed Shae. And Alex and Brody. And those sisters? The missing twins? Yeah, I killed them too."

Stu slapped his knee and burst into laughter. "That's a good one, Brit! Almost scared me for a minute."

My face didn't change. Stu's fell.

"Wait, you're-you're serious?"

"Yeah. They're not the first people I've killed either. I'm so sorry I hid this from you, but you can see why." I motioned to him. "You're a cop! I'm in love with a cop, and I knew I couldn't keep my secret from you. Stu, I love you. I want us to be together. This is why I said we couldn't be…" Tears stained my face.

Stu just stared at me, expressionless.

"Say something. Please?"

He stood and walked into the kitchen. I followed him. He pulled a beer from the fridge and chugged it. I sat at the table, head hung, still crying. Stu threw the bottle into the recycle bin.

"I gotta go," he said and walked out.

I didn't follow. I stayed on that chair until I fell asleep.

Thirty-One

THE NEXT MORNING, I woke with my head on the table and my eyes swollen. I had never been more grateful for a day I didn't have to work.

I tried to call Stu, but he didn't answer. I sent him texts, but he ignored those too. I wondered how long it would be until I heard from him again. Then I realized I might not. He's still a cop and I'm still a killer.

I put food out for Minion and trudged up to my bed, determined to allow myself the day to mourn my loss. But only today. No one could know that I fucked up this badly. I'd probably tell the girls that we had a fight about something small that erupted into him calling me a "scared little girl" and walking out. Yeah, that would work. They all knew that was true enough.

Minion joined me as I cried more. I fell asleep on and off until daybreak.

The sun shone into the bathroom and reflected off the sink. The one eye that I'd opened was momentarily blinded. I blinked a couple times and rolled from my warm spot.

I went about my morning routine as though nothing had changed. But everything had. I blew my world up and set it on fire. I still had Passing Through, and I still had the girls.

But I didn't have Stu. I had to accept the fact that he was lost to me forever.

No one showed up to arrest me last night and still not now. I was grateful he hadn't told anyone. Would he? I didn't think so. I knew he loved me. I just had to hope it was enough to keep my secret.

I got dressed and went for my morning jog. I was watching the bay when someone nearly knocked me over.

"Watch it, asshole!" I yelled.

"I'm so sorry!" The man looked at me, and recognition flashed in his eyes. "Britney? Is that you?"

"Andrew!" I playfully punched him in the bicep. "You're still an asshole for not paying attention. How are you?"

He slid closer in a pathetic attempt to kiss me.

I snorted in disgust, easing away from him. "Some things don't change," I said, putting my earbuds back in. I glanced at him once more, then jogged off.

He would die next.

Acknowledgments

This book, let alone series, wouldn't be possible without the following people and references:

Practical Homicide Investigation (5th Edition) by way of a Thomas Harris acknowledgement. The FBI's *Serial Murder Multi-Disciplinary Perspectives for Investigators* Report (available free online), and *psychologytoday.com* for helping me add the necessary depth to Britney.

Ret. Sgt. Chuck Burns for his consultation where the textbook didn't answer specific questions.

Justin D., for helping me on ridiculously short notice with some nicknames.

Nathan, for his advice and invitations. I'm so very grateful I finally decided to take you up.

Mark…sweet Mark. Without you, I wouldn't be here. I love you more than I can express and always will.

Jason, for the awesome editing and blurbs and feedback and advice and just being you. You have made me the writer I am today. Let's not get arrested, please. At least not before we make that money.

Also by
Amanda Byrd

13 Reasons for Murder:
Politeness Kills (#1)
Meathead (#2)
Philistines (#3)
Hungry (#4)
Bad Blood (#5)
Betrayal (#6)
Disillusioned (#7)

The Morgan Davis Serials
The Girl at the Bottom of the Ocean (#1)
Before You Die (#2)

Anthologies
Thrill of the Hunt: Cabin Fever (Thrill of the Hunt Anthology
Book 6)

The Dr. van Wolfe Saga
Trapped (book 1)
Moratorium (book 2)
Medicate (book 3)